Find Madigan!

Bronco Madigan was the top man in the US Marshals' Service – and now he was missing. Working on the most important and dangerous mission he'd ever been assigned, he'd disappeared into the gunsmoke.

Everything pointed to him being one of the dead bodies left along the bloody trail. Even his sidekick, Kimble, was almost ready to give up the search but the Chief's orders were very clear.

'Find Madigan . . . at all costs!'

Find Madigan!

Hank J. Kirby

A Black Horse Western

ROBERT HALE · LONDON

© Hank J. Kirby 2006
First published in Great Britain 2006

ISBN-10: 0-7090-8196-0
ISBN-13: 978-0-7090-8196-8

Robert Hale Limited
Clerkenwell House
Clerkenwell Green
London EC1R 0HT

The right of Hank J. Kirby to be identified as
author of this work has been asserted by him
in accordance with the Copyright, Designs and
Patents Act 1988

Typeset by
Derek Doyle & Associates, Shaw Heath
Printed and bound in Great Britain by
Antony Rowe Limited, Wiltshire

CHAPTER 1

RED CANYON

The rider in the faded pink shirt, plastered to his upper body with sweat and many miles of trail dirt, wasn't expecting the ambush quite so soon.

He figured they would wait until he had entered the tangle of red-rock canyons a mile or so to the east. But here he was, still negotiating the twisting trail up to the higher country from the pass and a rifle blasted from the needle rocks above and to his right.

The man up there was a pretty good shot but maybe the glare threw him, for the bullet went wide, but churned across a jutting hip of sandstone almost alongside his target's horse, then plunged in a corkscrew motion, driving into the black's body.

The rider felt the mount flinch and heard its whicker of pain and shock. The rear end swerved and collapsed a bit – and this saved him from the next shot which passed just over his head. He sprawled along the frightened horse's neck, dug in the spurs, reins twisted in one hand, the other sliding the Winchester from the saddle scabbard. The third shot ripped the pink shirt across his back and he flinched, feeling the burn of passing lead. He let his weight fall onto his right foot in the stirrup, swung up the rifle one-handed, seeing the gunsmoke up amongst the needles: in this breathless air it hung there like a flag marker.

The rifle bucked against his wrist and for a moment he thought he had lost his grip but he managed to hold on. He put the horse under the meagre cover of a broken ledge, watched lead from above chew the rock to dust and whirring flakes with razor edges.

Rifle held in two hands now, reins between his teeth, knees gripping the black, he brought the gun to his shoulder, held on the spot he knew the bush-whacker must appear if he wanted to shoot again.

There was his man! Edging out slow, in a blue checked shirt – which changed to blue-check-and-red as two bullets ploughed through the cloth, knocked the bushwhacker flat against a rock, exposing his upper body. The killer teetered, blood flooding his shirt front now, and the rider in the pink shirt added to it with his next blast from the Winchester.

The bushwhacker made no sound, but his body leaned out into space, toppled past the point of balance and bounced off the sloping ledge that protected the target and the injured black horse. The dead face of the killer was exposed as he fell. The rider nodded without surprise.

'Slick Carpenter! I might've known they'd give you the job!'

The body struck the slope, loosening shale and scree, a small dust cloud rising. Rifle reloaded, the man in the pink shirt warily edged the black out from under the ledge feeling for his Colt, which wasn't there. *Colorado never wore a six-gun so he had left his behind. . . .*

Crouched low, he scanned the rim above.He couldn't see any more riflemen but waited a full ten minutes before heeling the suffering black forward. Working the reins one-handed, rifle butt held against his thigh, he edged downslope, still watching the rim. He thought grimly, *looks like I'm finally on the right trail, but my cover's blown. Damnit!*

And they were smarter than he'd allowed: leastways the man they had picked as Carpenter's back-up was.

This second killer waited until the rider in the now-ragged and bloodstained pink shirt reached the flats that led into the tangled canyon country, waited until the man dismounted and stood at the black's bloody hip, examining the wound. The water from the rider's canteen was tepid and he gulped a mouthful first before pouring some over the blood-pulsing gash torn by the ricocheting bullet.

The flattened lead was still in there and must be hurting like hell. He knew he was going to have to cut it out if he was to continue looking for that son of a bitch who called himself Johnny True, otherwise the horse would be crippled, likely to die. There was no choice. The black was the only mount he had, but Carpenter must've had a horse! He could search and swap his saddle over and . . . no, he wasn't the kind of man to let any animal suffer, let alone a horse that had

7

served him so well these past weeks.

He decided to look for a tight little box canyon that he could fence off to make sure the black stayed put and didn't run far once the cutting was done. Moving his shoulders stiffly, for the gouge across his back was beginning to burn now, he said aloud, 'Gotta be done, or we're both dead.'

He dropped the canteen cork and stooped to pick it up just as a rifle whiplashed from the rock wall of the first canyon, a good 250 yards away.

It wasn't a Winchester: the sound was different, sharper, more powerful, and the bullet must be a big one for he heard the *thrumming* of its passing like a kid's notched whip-top just starting to spin. *Modified Springfield .45-.70.* He dropped the canteen. Paying no heed to the water spilling out, he grabbed the saddle horn, got one boot in the stirrup and yelled in the black's ear. The sudden closeness of the shout set it moving with a twisting, protesting motion.

Hanging on the side, keeping the black's sweating body between him and the shooter, he rode towards the canyon, not away as might be expected. The man was shooting from a long distance and almost certainly using a peep sight and Vernier scale. He would be all set to adjust for a longer shot, expecting the man in the pink shirt to ride away, but he was thrown when the man came closer. He fumbled the sight, cursing as he tried to reverse the adjustment. It flipped back down into its nesting groove. Frantically, he tried to erect it again with a horny thumbnail, desperate to get another shot at his target.

By then the rider was in the saddle and thrashing

the bleeding mount into the first of the snake-like passes through the canyons. He threw up his rifle, raked the killer's position with a long volley that would make him keep his head down.Then urged the horse on. No point in staying to fight: all the advantage was with the killer on the rim: height, steady position, fine weapon, large calibre.

So he lashed with the loose rein ends, hearing the grunting, gasping breaths of the struggling horse.The black wouldn't last much longer. He was losing too much blood and the hip working like it was would soon give out.

Then he heard the bellow of the killer gun again. At the same instant, the horse's head jerked wildly. The black started to twist around towards him, the eyes wild and white-rimmed, somehow accusing. He didn't hear the big gun thunder again, only knew a sensation of his hat being torn from his head and someone laying a red-hot poker across his skull, splitting it open.Pain shattered his brain. Liquid flashes and swirls distorted his vision in a ragged series of brilliant arcs. The world jarred and leapt insanely and disappeared in a blazing glare, rapidly replaced by engulfing blackness.

He was known as *Wakina* – Thunder in the language of the Lakota-Sioux. Some called him *Pahaska* – Long Hair – but he didn't mind. Long ago he had forgotten his white-man name – *chose* to forget it – and, as he was a loner, he saw few people to worry about who called him what.

Thunder originated not only from his bellowing voice – which he used on various occasions – but also from the long-barrelled Sharps Big Fifty rifle he carried to hunt the buffalo of the Great Plains.

He was a good hunter, paid a fair wage to the Indian women who scraped fat from the hides and the bucks who worked as skinners. They could choose silver or goods of their liking. He could travel in safety the length and breadth of the Indian lands and if it was true that he did indeed do this, year after year, season after season, and that he left behind a brood of children that could be numbered in their dozens, then it didn't bother him at all. Except maybe to stir a little pride in that massive chest.

Why, he must be into his sixties by this time. . . .

He could be a hard man as well as a good man: several had found this out over the years, but were no longer around to warn others that behind that booming voice and thunderous laughter, there was a heart as big as a buffalo's – and as cold as that of a diamondback rattler on occasion.

He was a man who strode through life to his own drumbeat and he could be kind, even soft-hearted, but he would not be bullied, or put-upon, or insulted and he would fight any man walking this earth who was foolish enough to try any of those things with him. Or his friends.

Life's endless problems and hassles never fazed him for long and mostly he managed to be self-sufficient. Just occasionally something beat that inventive mind and agile fingers and then the black mood would take him. There was a secret place known to no one but Wakina himself, a place where firewater straight from the lethal condensers of Hell itself could be found.

10

And when he drank this he was a fearsome man to behold and all those on the Great Plains who knew him, stayed well out of his way.

Even certain animals – cougar, rogue buffalo bulls, giant loping timber wolves – seemed to sense his inner raging and crept away to their own secret lairs, emerging only after he reappeared, sunken-eyed, gaunt, a sorry sight, but gentle as a lamb now the demons had been exorcised – until the next time.

That late fall day when he rode down out of the Tetons, his Big Fifty clutched in a gnarled hand so tightly it seemed as if he was trying to *strangle* the weapon, he could feel the stirring once more of those demons.

The damn gun was the cause of it! He wouldn't be here now except that the well-worn, well-used weapon had acted-up and brought him this way.

Well, actually, the – *thing* – had misfired twice when he was on a buffalo stand, picking off the best beasts, the ones already sporting the lush growth of fur in preparation for the coming winter. Coats and cloaks made from such hides were just as warm as those made from full-winter hides and only half the weight. This latter fact was much appreciated by ladies of fashion in the cities.

He was an expert at picking the animals with the best pre-winter's growth. He had taken great care reloading his cartridges, filing off the mould marks on the bullets, using an accurate ram's horn powder measure to give consistent loads, and reaming the cases with any nicks or dents in their mouths and necks. He scrubbed the entire weapon with soap-bark suds, oiled the working parts, cut strips of buckskin to keep handy for cleaning the heavy barrel's rifling, adjusted the trigger let-off just right – not too hard that would require a jerk, nor too light that would fire prematurely and so miss the target. Or only wound it.

All went well on the first stand at Crazy Woman Creek in the foothills, then, out on the Plains, at the hidden patch of sweet grass he had discovered last year. Here he found a herd that was plump, hides and horns glistening, contentedly feeding, and he settled in to make his fortune.

He was getting old and he needed to stash away some money for when his rheumatism and old bone-breaks that had never healed properly in the wilds would prevent him from hunting well enough to make a living. Of course, he had told himself this every year for the past ten years and still he had nothing more to show for his resolve than a couple of quarters and maybe a half-dollar in his pockets.

But this time the damn Big Fifty let him down!

The trigger was perfect, fired just at the right moment, but more than once the pin did not drive into the percussion cap hard enough to fire the cartridge. And that was disaster. For while a man could pick off buffalo a dozen at a time as they grazed without spooking the herd or even causing much interest from the other animals as their companions dropped around them – the cocking and clicking of a gun hammer, or the even quieter *snap!* of a firing pin being driven home, could cause them to scatter like leaves in the wind. In all his years of hunting buff, Wakina had never figured out the why of this, nor could any of his Indian friends give a satisfactory explanation.

It is the way of the Great Spirit – their answer for most things mysterious.

So, he drove off two small herds and wondered why the Creator made such capricious animals as bison! Finally the sweet-grass herd bounded away after his third shot – the shot that never happened. The one just before it, too, had kind of *sizzled* rather than fired with full charge and he had ended up only wounding the herd leader – a cow, with a pale golden ruff of fur that tantalized him and raised his ire to murderous levels.

But he managed to control his anger as he tracked it down across the plains and through the foothills, blood spoor growing darker, and he knew he *had* to find this buffalo. Not for the golden collar of fur, but to put the animal out of its misery. He prided himself that he had never let an animal die in agony from any wound he had inflicted: he would abandon everything else in his track-down until he could deliver the final, humane shot that would end the beast's suffering.

And so he tracked the cow buffalo down into a hollow at the edge of a grassless plain. It was down on its knees by then, unable to rise up to continue its painful journey to wherever its devils were driving it. Blood hung in black tendrils from its mouth and nostrils. The large bovine eyes were sunken and dulling, the wound already fly-blown.

Grimly, Wakina loaded the Sharps, chose his best cartridge and walked up to within six feet of the downed buffalo. She stared at him, tried to bellow, but the choking, rasping noise brought prickles to his skin as fresh blood gushed and he raised the big rifle swiftly and squeezed the trigger.

For once the weapon responded, its bellowing roar jumping back from the hills. The heavy bullet drove in between those pathetic, pain-filled eyes, the impact jerking the drooping head hard enough to crack the neck.

The golden ruff was soiled with blood and dirt and he decided he would not defile the animal any more. It seemed a shame to leave it to the crows and buzzards, but he could never take it, or sell it. It had not been won fairly the way he looked at it.

The rough-tough giant in soiled buckskins was just an old softy at heart. But he still had to do something about the Sharps. He was an amateur gunsmith, but this problem was beyond him. It was inconsistent in performance and that was not good enough by a long, long country mile for a man who made his living by the gun.

So he decided that as he had come this far south and east, he would continue on to Fort Fremont in the Wind River Range and have the weapon checked by a professional.

The decision took him back slightly into the Teton Foothills and while climbing a trail over a rise, he paused to hunt up a chaw of tobacco in one of the greasy pockets of his stained buckskins. Holding it in both hands after brushing it off on his jacket, he chomped down with his big yellow teeth – the four remaining front ones, anyway – and wrenched his head back and forth in an effort to tear off a hunk he could work around his gums.

Twice when his head twisted he caught a glimpse of

something to his right and below, in a hollow with broken edges. Standing in his stirrups, shading his eyes that after fifty years of roaming the wilderness were finally beginning to cloud over, he forgot he had a chunk of tobacco in his mouth and spat. It flew out with saliva and landed in a tolerably fresh pile of manure – looked like mountain cat to him. But he swore only briefly and looked again.

'Hoss down,' he muttered in his raspy rumbling voice. 'An' – what in *hell* is that? A man? Yeah, Wakina, you can still see well enough to say it's a man. Not only that, he – he's wearin' a pink shirt – *pink*, for the love of Mike! What kinda man would wear *pink* in this country?'

He shook his head in disbelief, started to lower his shading hand, checked, and squinted again, long and hard.

'Well, I do believe that pretty damn dude shirt is spattered with blood!' He eased back in the saddle and kicked his heels into the flanks of his lean, muscular sorrel. 'Sweetheart, you an' me had best get on down there. If that feller's sufferin' like the buffalo cow, well, I won't need the Sharps to put him outa his misery – just my ol' skinnin' knife. Ain't gonna waste a bullet on him whoever he is.'

As he rode out towards the unmoving man and the obviously dead horse, he saw the buzzards riding the thermals down against the blue fall sky, beginning to spiral towards their target.

It would be touch and go who reached the man in the pink shirt first – old Thunder or the carrion birds with their insatiable hunger and eager beaks and talons.

CHAPTER 2

WHERE'S MADIGAN?

Miles Parminter, Chief US Federal Marshal, couldn't concentrate on the boring routine forms that seemed to gather on his desk in thicker and thicker piles each week.

They had to be done, by *him*, it had been decreed by someone in Congress, who must surely have some terrible grudge to settle, condemning him to this drudgery week by week.

There was so much had to be done out there in the field, dammit! He had operatives working all over the country: some had to be tracked and chaperoned from afar while they gained experience; others had to be curtailed in their enthusiasm, brought into line so their actions were within the law – that way, when it came to court, they were more likely to get a conviction.

And there were some who were mavericks.

16

Men who made their own rules, stepped outside the law, dispensed justice with a six-gun when they knew they had the law-breaker dead-to-rights, but who for one reason or another, would never be brought to heel by the justice system.

These were the men he nurtured most, though no one would ever guess this from the scathing reports and harsh disciplinary actions he dispensed to the miscreants – on paper, anyway.

He knew the men who gave him the most trouble this way were the best men he had working for him. Dedicated deputy marshals, long experienced, knowing the law and how it could be manipulated by trangressors who paid high-flying attorneys to delay court hearings – or, with a little more luck (and perhaps a lot more money) have the charges thrown out entirely.

The only way then was for 'justice' to take the shape of a bullet. He never openly condoned this, of course.

'To hell with this!' Parminter said suddenly, shoving the papers he had been working on into a nearby pile which collapsed and shed its forms in a slithering cascade onto the floor of his office. A big man with cropped hair, his round, rugged face flushed and his chest swelled with rising anger, he stood, and growled, '*Aaagh!*' and let it go at that, walking over the spilled forms and leaving the dusty imprint of his boot soles behind. He wrenched open the door as if he would yank it off its hinges, bellowed, 'Milt!'

A clerk sitting at one of the three desks in the room was already on his feet, snatching a notebook and pencil, hurrying towards Parminter filling the doorway of his office. He made no attempt to move aside and Milt frowned, slowed, perplexed.

'Yes, Marshal. . . ?' he asked tentatively, his stomach knotting up when he saw the thunder on the Old Man's face.

'You know what I'm going to ask!'

Milt flinched. 'Er – I'm not sure. . . .'

'Damn you! Tell me! *Is there any word yet* from Bronco Madigan! It's two weeks since I last heard. . . .'

Milt tried a crooked smile – without a lot of success. 'Well, you know Madigan, Marshal, he's a law unto himself.'

'Shove the platitudes in your bottom drawer, damnit! You answer my question!'

Milt swallowed and shook his head slowly. 'I'm sorry, Marshal, no word yet. I've sent a wire to Cassidy and he's trying to get a line on Bronco's last sighting but we're not even sure it was him.'

'Christ! That should've been done a week ago.'

Milt flushed, shocked. 'Now be fair, sir! Two weeks out of contact is allowable before we—'

'*One week!* I've just changed the rules! Now you follow through on that right away, Milt! This – this is probably the most important – and most dangerous – case Madigan has ever had. And because Kimble's still pussyfooting around on that kidnap deal up in Wisconsin, Bren had to take on the case alone, without back-up.'

Milt was making brief notes on his pad. Parminter stopped.

'Milt,' he said very quietly and the clerk stiffened instantly, eyes coming up full of apprehension. 'Why're you still standing here, scrawling on that pad,

18

instead of hot-footing it down to the messengers' department, following through on my orders?'

Milt nodded, muttered, almost dropped his notepad and then was hurrying down past the other two conscientious-looking clerks when Parminter called.

'Milt, see if you can track down Kimble, too, but nothing has priority over finding Madigan. Understand?'

'Yes, Marshal. Find Madigan, top priority.'

Parminter went back into his office, glared at the mess of paper and kicked it on his way to a cupboard. He took out a crystal decanter and poured himself a stiff bourbon.

It was unusual for him to drink during working hours but he felt unusual – *mighty* unusual. He had been a man in the field himself and had worked his way up. He knew the things that could happen to an operative out there, knew the hundreds of acceptable reasons for delay in keeping contact with head office, too.

But this time – *this time!* – he had a gut-feeling that was wrenching him apart. It had started three days ago, in the middle of the night. The notion – no, the *fear* – had hit him like a kick in the belly from a mule.

Something had happened to Bronco Madigan, his top man. Something had happened – something bad!

He knew well enough that anxiety such as this was unproductive and most times was unnecessary, especially with a maverick of Madigan's expertise. And that was precisely why he gave the hunch so much attention this time.

Because it refused to go away. And the days dragged on with no word, no sign, even of that bastard Johnny True, likely the most dangerous son of a bitch the marshal's office had ever come up against. *Find True, find Madigan!*

'If you've somehow managed to kill Madigan. . . .' Parminter gritted aloud. He paused, threw down another hefty slug of bourbon.

He didn't want to pursue that line of thought.

He sat down, staring soberly into the amber liquid.

'Goddamnit, Bren! Where the hell are you?'

Deputy United States Marshal Beaumont T. Kimble was naked under the sheets when Priscilla, half-clutching a velvety robe about her lithe body, came back into the bedroom and told him there was a man asking for him.

Kimble's hair was all awry and he pushed some back from his eyes, looking at her sharply, not, at this moment, fully appreciating the glimpse of curving bosom and silky thighs as she adjusted the gown in the cold room.

'You didn't say I was here?'

She pouted, her red hair flying as she tossed her head. 'He already *knew* you were here! What choice did I have? There's sleet outside and the man is absolutely frozen—'

He groaned. 'You didn't ask him in?'

'Of course I did! Good manners could never dictate otherwise.'

'Hell almighty,' Kimble breathed as he had heard Bronco Madigan do many times when frustrated or surprised. And at the moment he was both. Things had been getting mighty interesting in the bed when the urgent rap had come to the door. With Priscilla's parents and all the staff except one maid having gone south for the winter the next two or three days had promised to be paradise.

'In the kitchen, I suppose?' he asked, bitterly, as he swung long legs over the side of the bed.

She looked a little regretful, glimpsing that young, taut-muscled body with the two small scars, nodded and said, simultaneously with the marshal, 'Having hot coffee . . .' She hurriedly added, 'Oh, Beau, the poor man's absolutely frozen! I – I just had to. . . .'

Kimble was half dressed now, hopped across the room on one leg as he tried to pull on one of his boots and planted a passing kiss on her ivory face. She instinctively reached for him to add some substance to the kiss but he staggered on by and found his other boot under a chair.

By the time he was dressed – more or less decently, though hair still ruffled – she stood with both hands on her hips after tugging the gown tightly closed all the way up to her neck. 'You didn't have to get fully dressed!' she snapped.

'Yes, I did, my sweet. Only two people apart from you know I am here and neither would rattle my spurs unless it was mighty important.'

'Oh! You – you're beginning to sound more like a Westerner every time I see you! This – this Madigan you work for—'

'Not *for*: as his sidekick,' he answered, with a crooked, maddening smile but got nothing back, except a tightening of those red lips.

'There you go again! Oh, damn you, Beau Kimble! You never used to be like this when you lived here in Norfolk, once one of the young bucks of Virginian Society, but now— Oh, go see what your damn messenger wants ! But don't expect to find me waiting here with open arms!'

'Sure you will. Just don't lose the place!' One of her slippers clattered against the door as he dashed out.

He recognized the man in the kitchen as he waited for a refill of his coffee cup from Jessica, the servant woman. She looked a query at Kimble and he nodded. They remained silent while she poured him a cup, too, and then left the warmth of the big room.

'First time I been in a real mansion,' the messenger said. 'You hear plenty of stories around town about what goes on here behind them big carved doors but this is—'

'What brings you here, Mac?' interrupted Kimble beginning to feel a little riled now.

'Orders from Chief Parminter, Beau – Madigan's missin'. Chief wants you back in Washington pronto.'

'Bronco? How long's he been missing?'

'Couple weeks since they heard from him. . . .'

Kimble swore softly – a bad habit he had picked up working with Bronco Madigan. 'Good God, what're they worried about? If Bronco's onto a hot trail it'll be nothing if six weeks pass before he checks in, or shows up in the chief's office with the case solved and a string of dead men stretching into infinity behind him!'

Mac, a thin man who seemed to be only wearing a

slicker over shirt and trousers, shivered once and sipped some more coffee. 'Parminter's real upset. Somethin's stuck in his craw. Snappin' everyone's head off. Ain't like him.'

Kimble frowned. 'Mmm. Maybe he knows more than he's saying. Maybe there *has* been some word about Bronco, but he's keeping it to himself for some reason. . . .'

'Till you get back, eh?' suggested Mac.

Kimble's face straightened slowly. 'By God! I know he was working on something mighty important . . . no details. The chief played it very close to his chest, more so than usual.'

'They want you back there fast, Beau.'

Kimble sighed, thinking with rising bitterness, and here I've wound up the case I was on and, instead of reporting back right away, I decided to stop off and indulge myself for a few days with an old flame, while Madigan could be. . . . He snapped his head up abruptly.

'Mac, book me a seat – first class – on the night train to Washington. I'll pick up the ticket at the depot.'

'I could bring it back here for you,' Mac said, hopefully.

'You could, but you're not going to. Now get moving – you've got enough free coffee inside you to see you through the sleet to the depot.' He fumbled a coin out of pocket and flicked it to the man. 'Have something stronger to warm your innards, but *after* you book my seat on the train.'

Mac caught the coin expertly and grinned as he grabbed his sodden hat from the back of a chair nearer the glowing wood range.

'You ain't been with Madigan long enough to pick up all of his good ways, yet! *He* wouldn't expect me to go out in that storm so soon.' He held up the coin briefly. 'But you're not doin' too bad! Have a good night, Beau!'

As soon as he had left, Beaumont T. Kimble hurried along to Priscilla's suite of rooms. He was pleasantly surprised to find her in bed with the covers pulled right up under her chin, the red hair spilled across the pillow. He grinned as he stepped inside, locking the door behind him.

'Er, I have a few hours to wait for my train back to Washington.' His smile widened as he saw the velvety gown draped over the foot of the feather bed.

Priscilla's slanting green eyes flickered mischievously. 'Well, aren't you lucky!'

'Someone is!' Kimble was already disrobing and, when he was stark naked and tiptoeing to the bed, teeth chattering, she flung the covers aside and he stared, jaw dropping, eyes wide.

She was fully dressed – and slipped out of bed as he gaped. She smiled at him. 'I've decided to go riding.'

'In this storm?' He was aghast, frozen in the act of climbing into the bed on his side.

She shrugged indifferently, moving very swiftly, now, scooping up his clothes as she ran out the door. Legs tangled in the bedclothes, he started to panic when he heard the key turn in the lock – on the outside. He ran to the door, pounded on it with his fists.

'Prissy! *Priscilla!* Unlock this door at once!'

'Sorry, Beau. Can't wait now. Oh, Jessica will be

24

coming with me. You'll have the place all to yourself, so you can catch up on some of that sleep you planned to lose tonight but did nothing about! 'Bye! Sleep tight!'

He groaned and, shivering violently now, ran back to the bed, pulling the covers over him.

If he missed that night train to Washington. . . !

Kimble didn't dare contemplate the consequences.

The shadow blotting out the sun made the wounded man open his eyes.He had been lying here – wherever *here* was – for maybe ten minutes, wondering what had happened to him, and why was he lying on some sort of animal skin? His head throbbed with shattering pain. But it wasn't like a hangover – leastways, none that he remembered.

He felt like he was wearing a hat, something firm, but not tight, across his forehead and around the back of his skull.Then the shadow darkened his closed eyelids and they snapped open as he exclaimed, 'Jesus Christ! Who the hell is that?'

If the shock of seeing a veritable giant with long hair and battered face leaning over him had shaken him, he was literally rocked to his toes as a hand the size of a horse's hoof smacked him across the side of the head. A large finger, like a sausage, waved in front of his face. He tried to focus his rolling eyes upon it as a booming voice said, 'Swear if you want, pilgrim, but take not the Lord's name in vain within my hearin', or you could get to meet him quicker than you reckon on!'

He blinked, head thundering. The man straightened a little, sitting back on his hams. Even squatting like that he was huge. 'What be your name, pilgrim?'

The man with the bandaged head squinted and opened his mouth to speak, but closed it again, sat in silence for a moment, then said, tight-lipped, 'My name don't matter. Who the hell're you and where am I?'

'I am called Wakina – that's Lakota for Thunder, and perhaps the sweet and gentle timbre of my voice will give you a clue as to how I earned the name. My other name is Pahaska, he of the long hair.' The big fist tugged at some greasy, shoulder-length locks. 'And you be in my camp, temporary though it is. You have been shot in the head and a couple of other places but they matter little. 'Tis the head wound that bothers me.'

'Bothers you?' A shaky hand reached up and touched the bandage wrapped around his head. He blinked, trying to clear clouded vision. He could make out, hazily, a rockface of reddish stone veined with grey, and a horse, only partly seen. There was a deal of saddle gear piled off to one side. 'Where's this camp?'

'Not far from where I found you – just outside Red Canyon. You recall. . . ?'

The wounded man frowned. 'I— Things are a mite hazy right now – Red Canyon. . . ?'

'Edge of the Tetons – Wyoming.' Wakina watched closely, saw the man struggling to make sense of his words. 'Your horse had brought you far, gallantly, I'd say, with two or three bullets in him, before he collapsed. You were lucky I saw you when I did. Just beat a couple of dozen buzzards to you. It'll all come back to you later.'

The man stared blankly, then nodded slightly. 'I know . . . buzzards. . . .'

'You have enemies, my friend. I checked the canyons, found a couple of piles of empty brass rifle shells – a goodly distance apart. You put up a fight, I think, but the sign reads that you were ambushed.'

Again he waited but the wounded man gave no reaction. 'You've been most of the day comin' round. I'm on my way to Fort Fremont, but didn't want to move you while you were still unconscious.' The old buffalo hunter's eye sharpened and he leaned closer. 'You don't know your name, do you?'

The man reacted with a jerk that trembled through his entire body. It was a rangy body and, stripped to the waist as he was, showed scars from old bullet wounds, and criss-crossed ridges on his back that could only have been left by a whip's whistling coils. He was about forty, Wakina guessed, had led a hard life, but was well up to meeting adversity and better-ing it – or coming to terms with it. There were dark marks on his whipcord trousers where he had worn his gunbelt and although he hadn't had it when found, these marks told the old hunter that the holster had been tied down low on the thigh. The ball of the right thumb had a callous, too. Wakina knew well the marks a gun hammer left on human skin: his own right thumb sported a much bigger callous than the other man's. There was a place inside one of the boots for a slim knife blade – missing – and in the other, a holster for a small derringer pistol, also miss-ing.

27

It was Wakina's judgement that here was a man who had lived violently and had almost died the same way.

The wounded man reached up and felt the bandages again, and there was a haunted look far back in his dark eyes. The old hunter spoke more quietly now, though the voice still tended to boom into the rapidly closing evening.

'I'll take you to a sawbones at the fort if you wish, but I have doctored the head wound and I believe it will heal well in a couple of weeks – at least, on the outside.' His eyes bored into the man's face again. 'You have forgotten your name, haven't you, pilgrim?' He asked the question quietly this time with genuine compassion replacing earlier mockery.

The man's jaw jutted a little. He looked defiant despite his haggard face. Then his shoulders slumped and he nodded. There was both resignation and sadness in his voice when he spoke.

'Wakina, I dunno who I am. There's just . . . emptiness! Nothing!'

There was a touch of rising panic in the harshly delivered words, and a kind of fear flared in the haunted eyes.

Here was a man who was lost – literally – riding the Limbo Line with nowhere to go, nowhere to retreat. A man who, through no fault of his own, had just gone missing from the world he had once known.

CHAPTER 3

NEW MAN

'Vance. That's a name I've always been partial to. How say you, pilgrim? Would you like to be a "Vance"?'

The man with the head bandage looked up from where he was casually examining Wakina's Sharps buffalo rifle and after a long moment asked, 'First name or last?'

'Why, it hardly matters, does it? "Someone" Vance or Vance "Someone". I believe the choice to be yours.'

After another long stare the man nodded. ' "Vance" it is.'

'It doesn't stir anythin' else? Make you think of another name or—?'

'Nothing. It's just a word in a big black, deep pool – Maybe I'll fill it up with something worthwhile, but for now Vance is a lone star in an empty universe.'

'You speak better than most Westerners, pilgrim. It could be you've had some kind of education.'

'Well, it hasn't done me much good if I don't even remember my own name.'

Wakina pursed his leathery old lips. 'Pilgrim – Vance – I know little of this problem that now afflicts you, but it is my belief that you will do better to cast out whatever bitterness you may be feelin'.'

Vance smiled crookedly. 'No *may be* about it, *amigo*. You figure you wouldn't be bitter?'

'That I can not answer but – *amigo*? A Spanish word, pilgrim – remember it. There could be a clue there. Aye, you will have to snatch at crumbs, stow 'em away until you have enough for your memory to feed upon, and gain that nourishment you crave.'

'You talk kinda queer.'

The laugh was as thunderous as Wakina's voice and echoed through the early morning mist. 'I come from religious stock, pilgrim – believe it or not. My reverend father was always practising his sermons in a great booming voice so he could "project" to all parts of the churches where he preached. I seem to have inherited his voice as well as his manner of speech. I trust it does not offend you?'

Vance smiled again, shook his head gently, wincing slightly. 'Hell, no. There's nothing you could do to offend me, Thunder, not after saving my life.'

The old hunter nodded soberly. 'My deed is not yet complete, though. You are a lost soul, drifting in a kind of memory limbo. I saved your life, so therefore I am obligated also to return your memory to you – if I can – give you back that life I saved you for.'

Vance studied him soberly. 'You are an odd one, and I don't mean that insultingly. But consider this: maybe the life I had before holds no interest for me now; maybe I am content with just the *here and now*.'

'Vance, you could not say that with any certainty unless you already recall your other life.'

Vance sighed. 'It was just a thought. No idea where it came from, but, OK, for now I'm Vance and here with you – and you've a gun that needs attention.'

Wakina was mildly surprised at the sudden change of subject but was willing to go along with it. 'It is the damnedest thing. Sometimes it fires perfectly, but at others – always when I have the perfect shot at the perfect target – it misbehaves. Maybe a misfire, maybe a partial fire – by that I mean. . . .'

'That it seems like the powder doesn't all burn or you are firing with a short load.'

'That I will guarantee does not happen – I measure each charge exactly.' Wakina narrowed his gaze at Vance. 'You would appear to know something about guns – a gunsmith, perhaps?'

Vance started to take the Sharps' action apart, using an eating knife as a screwdriver. He shrugged. 'Who knows. Don't ask me where any of this comes from, but I have a picture, a hazy one, somewhere in here.' He tapped his forehead, gently, for his whole head was still mighty sore. 'I think your trouble lies in the hammer spring.'

'I think not, pilgrim. I have examined it closely. It is a "Z"-shaped flat metal spring and is very easy to compress and to spring back to shape.'

'But how fast and how strongly does it spring back?' Vance had the cover plate off now and saw the spring in the exposed works. He cocked the hammer by the spur, watched the arms of the spring compress and come back into place when he tripped the trigger.

31

'The spring has lost much of its temper.'

Wakina hesitated, then conceded slowly, 'That could very well be so, pilgrim. It has had a lot of use. . . . This means I'll have to traipse all the way to Fremont after all and have a gunsmith make me a new one. Damn!'

'I can re-temper this one, harden the steel at least – provided you've got some sugar?'

'I have sugar. . . .' Wakina – 'Old Thunder' as he was more commonly known by white people – was puzzled.

'We need a hot fire and good set of coals.'

Wakina was taking a chance: this stranger might know what he was talking about, then again he might *not*. If the latter he would lose a spring and his gun would be useless and he would have to ride all the way to Fort Fremont to order new parts. On the other hand, if Vance *did* know what he was about, even though he did not know his own name . . . 'We'll give it a try, pilgrim. You are in charge.'

The spring was heated slowly until it became red, then mottled. Vance pulled it from the coals with a split green stick and on a flat rock he had prepared, sprinkled sugar crystals over the hot metal. They sizzled and flashed and caramelized as the heat and carbon in the crystals changed the molecular structure of the steel, hissing and bubbling. After a few moments, Vance plunged the spring first into cooking grease, then cold water.

As the steam evaporated, he dropped the Z-shaped spring onto the flat rock again. It rang, and bounced a little, whereas before it had only clattered dully.

Wakina's fingers were calloused enough for him to pick it up without the retained heat bothering him. He flicked the metal with a horny nail. Again that mild ringing tone. There was surprise in his voice.

'Pilgrim, I believe you have improved the temper a hundred per cent. I did not know that trick with the sugar.'

Vance frowned. 'Works on a knife, too, so it holds its edge longer. I dunno why it does it. Maybe I did once, maybe someone showed me.' He seemed to turn inward, searching inside himself, looking for an answer.

Wakina showed concern. 'Friend, don't allow this affliction of yours to stop you in your tracks. Accept the knowledge as a gift – utilize it and try to retain it. You will have to gather such things anew, learn to store them away so they can be recalled, and one day, the Good Lord may be merciful and include your true name.'

Vance's face was sober. 'I don't think me and the Lord've ever been on such good terms . . .' He dodged the back handed blow Wakina casually swung at him. He added swiftly, 'I wasn't bein' smart, damnit, Thunder! I wasn't even aware of what I was going to say – it just – came.'

'All right, pilgrim. But it is a touchy subject with me. Forced training by my father. Perhaps one day I will tell you about him if you stay with me long enough.'

Vance's head came up. 'Are you asking me to stay with you?'

'Where can you go? Oh, I know you could manage. You are self-sufficient, that is abundantly clear, but you show signs that this loss of memory has hit you a lot harder than you mean to disclose. The years are catchin' up with me and they ain't been all that kind. My eyes are cloudy, my joints ache with the rheumatiz even in summer; I creak some morns when I mount my saddle. I have yet to make enough money to ease my life into my winter years. So you see, I am being selfish askin' you to stay – a man who knows guns like you, who fought off ambushers. I neglected to tell you that in my search of the Red Canyon, I found two dead men, one with well-placed bullets in him, t'other torn by ricochet.'

'You figure I killed 'em?'

The huge shoulders moved a little as the long arms spread. 'I can see no other explanation.'

'I dunno buffalo hunting.'

'How can you be sure? You will learn quickly, I am sure of that. We can do well this season. I know where a big herd winters and with both of us hunting – I have another Sharps, a carbine, at my camp, as well as a Remington rolling-block for back-up. . . .'

'A Remington rolling-block?' There was real interest im Vance's voice. 'I wouldn't mind trying my hand with that!'

Wakina smiled thinly. 'Ah, pilgrim, it seems that anything to do with firearms stirs your interest and brings memories to the fore! It is my belief we can make this a fortunate partnership – in more ways than one. For you.'

Vance felt the clenching of his heart and a faint wave of dizziness washing through his brain.

By God! There did *seem to be some kind of a chance here*

for the taking. If he was game enough.

But anything would be better than this walking the edge of oblivion! 'Shake on it, Thunder, we have us a deal.'

Kimble felt sheepish as he faced the silent Parminter across the chief marshal's desk. The big man did not look up from the paper he was reading. Kimble waited.

And he knew that whatever the chief was going to say was likely to be a lot more than just 'Welcome back'.

He was right. Parminter signed the paper, then sat back in his chair, looking at the young deputy for the first time. His eyes were like bullets. Kimble swallowed, knowing he was the target. And deserved whatever was coming.

'You missed the night train, I hear, out of *Norfolk!* Which seems to be far from where you last reported in.'

'Marshal, I-I'm sorry, I'm fully at fault. The . . . the kidnap case was wound up much faster than expected.'

Parminter continued to stare and Kimble's words trailed off a little. 'The report I had said you arranged the ransom pay-off but somehow turned the tables and in the resulting shoot-out all the kidnappers were killed.'

'Yessir, but Miss Vandemere was completely unharmed,' Kimble spoke quickly.

Parminter seemed unimpressed. Then he said, gaze unwavering, 'Almost worthy of Bren Madigan – the kind of thing he would do. Risking everyone's life – including his own.'

'It was a calculated risk, sir, and – well, I have picked up some of Madigan's style since working with him.'

'*Some*, yes, but Madigan would have seen Miss Vandemere back to her parents safely before *taking unofficial leave!* You spent three whole days at Norfolk!'

Kimble was shaken that Parminter knew so much and tried his best to justify his erotic interlude with Miss Priscilla. 'Miss Vandemere was picked up by her brother as we neared Norfolk, sir.'

'Your job was to see her safely *home!* That means taking her right into her house, into her parents' presence and answering any of their questions before even contemplating your own – comforts!'

'But, her brother—'

'You should know your duty by now, Deputy Kimble. You could have been back here at least two days ago when your presence would have been of some use.'

'Sir, I didn't know—'

'Seeing as you didn't bother to report in, how could you?' Parminter was on his feet now, face darkening. 'Bren Madigan is missing!'

'Yes, Mac told me, but with Madigan, a couple of weeks is nothing to get alarmed about.'

Parminter seemed likely to explode but got control and sat down slowly, waving a hand towards a chair in front of his desk. 'Sit down, Beau,' he said mildly and when the wary deputy had done so, the chief marshal lit one of his cheroots and placed his elbows on his desk. 'You have heard of a man who calls himself

36

"John True"?'

'Vaguely. Some sort of outlaw on the West Coast? A killer-for-hire?'

'Exactly! A killer-for-hire. Too sophisticated to be called a "hired gun", a man with a vast opinion of himself and his importance in this world, and his obsession with perfection in his work.'

Kimble squirmed a little. 'I didn't know he was that big.'

Parminter snorted. '*He* thinks he is. To me, he's just another murderer who trades men's lives for money, with the protection of people in high places. Which is how he has been able to operate for so long with apparent immunity.'

Kimble had an aching feeling in his belly. 'Don't tell me he's here! In Washington!'

Parminter chuckled but without mirth. 'I wish like hell he was! We'd soon run the son of a bitch to ground. But, no, he's not here. We don't know where he is, but we do know he is on the loose and being paid the biggest fee he's ever earned. You know what that means?'

Kimble nodded. 'He's after a big target. A job that entails a lot of danger and he's raised his fee accordingly.'

'Suppose I tell you the fee is a half-a-million dollars?'

Kimble felt his eyes start against their sockets. His voice was little more than an exhalation of breath. 'A half-*million!* Surely that's an exaggeration, Chief—?'

Parminter's mouth was a razor slash. 'I don't exaggerate, Beau! Never mind why I'm so sure the information is correct. I am sure, and it means this to me: a man who asks that much money for one job, does so for only one reason: he knows he will never be able to work ever again at his profession. He will never be able to use his own identity, will have to spend a goodly portion of that fee arranging his own protection and security for the rest of his days.'

Kimble took a few moments to digest this. 'What kind of job would it be? I mean, you indicated this True is egotistical. If he pulls off a job of the magnitude you believe this will be and then goes into hiding. . . ? Surely that's not in character.'

Parminter's smile was twisted. 'The mistake everyone who knows about this – and there are very few – has made. Johnny True will not have to boast about his accomplishment, whatever it is. It will be so big everyone will talk about it, possibly for years. All he has to do is live his life of luxury and bask in the awe people will hold him in. The name "Johnny True" will be everywhere, even if he's using an entirely different one by that time. It will be enough for him, fame without revelation: that's the kind of ego Mr Goddamn True is capable of. Why, the man practically kisses himself good night!'

Kimble absorbed this and took his time about lighting one of his own cheroots before speaking. 'You obviously know him well, Chief.'

He was surprised when Parminter sat back and smiled – and shook his head. 'Never met the man. His reputation has been a thorn in the side of every Federal lawman for years. None of us knew where he was going to strike next. Some rumours have it that he has been in Europe, perhaps setting up his hide-away for when he completes this present job.'

'We have to find out what it is and stop him, is that the assignment, Chief?'

Parminter's face was cold. 'D'you think I would give such an assignment to someone with your limited experience, Beau? Even though you've had the best tutor in the service?'

Beau Kimble flushed, realizing he had spoken out of turn. 'I meant the service, Chief, when I said *we.*'

'Of course you did.' He leaned forward now. 'I gave the assignment to Bren Madigan. It is a chore that calls for Madigan's unorthodox approach – and, damnit, it was working! Or seemed to be until he disappeared. . . .'

Kimble blew out his cheeks. 'I see now why you're concerned at not hearing from Bronco. Two weeks on a normal assignment wouldn't be any cause for alarm, but on something as big as this. . . .'

The chief marshal stood, took a turn around his desk. He paused in front of the cabinet that contained his bourbon, but kept walking: this was not the time for alcohol.

'We've had little to go on. Word came in by Deputy Warren some weeks ago. Madigan had stopped him along the trail, sent his message to say he had found a lead he thought would take him right to Johnny True himself – might need back-up and we should have a group of our best guns standing by. He seemed in a desperate hurry and Warren got no more out of him. But he did learn that Madigan had apparently gone deep undercover and was using a false name and a reputation as a hired gun . . . it's easy to see what he had in mind.'

'Yes, he was going to join some outfit that was either in contact with True or would be soon. A mighty dangerous move, Chief!'

'But typical of Madigan. He told Warren he would make contact with this office in another week, at the latest – that was over two weeks ago now. *That* is why I am concerned for his safety. If they tumbled to him. . . .'

Kimble knew it wasn't likely. Madigan did some dangerous things but he was always mighty careful. Still, the man had been complaining about old wounds and age overtaking him on the last assignment they had done together. Was it possible that Madigan was *slipping*? Had he been careless? He had been mighty weary, which was understandable, for Parminter worked him endlessly: no sooner was one assignment over than he was sent out on another: even a man like Madigan could take only so much.

Beau stopped the line of thought as another, mighty uncomfortable one, slid into his mind:

He had been enjoying the charms of Miss Priscilla when he should have been back here, ready for another assignment while Madigan was in mortal danger. Starting two or three days earlier might have made the difference between life and death – for Madigan.

He felt himself flush at the thought and the flush deepened when he caught Parminter watching him

The Old Man knew what he was thinking.

'You've worked with him closer than anyone else, Beau. You should know what moves he might make, even where he'll go, in general.'

'Well, Chief, I don't really know Bronco that well. He plays things mighty close to his chest.'

'Which is why he's lived so long. Beau, your assignment is simple: see Warren, get every scrap of information out of him you can – there's bound to be something he isn't even aware of knowing – then outfit yourself with everything you think you'll need – *everything*: I'll authorize it.'

Parminter was standing in front of Kimble's chair now and the worried deputy had to tilt his head to look at him.

'Then *go find Madigan!*'

CHAPTER 4

BADMEN

Once again Vance looked at the crumpled, torn, bloodstained pink shirt that Thunder had crammed into his saddle-bags before leaving the Red Canyon country.

They had travelled through the Tetons, the old hunter riding on ahead and scouting, aware that the wounded man with him might still have enemies searching for him in these hills. But they had made it through in a few days and were now back at Thunder's camp. There were Indians who had been working on the downed buffalo he had left behind when he had set out to track the wounded cow.

Skinning, defatting and salting had progressed well.

'You must pay 'em well,' Vance said, indicating the industrious Indians. 'Working when you're not here.'

'Well enough, pilgrim. They show me loyalty – perhaps because at times I become one of them.' He laughed at the enquiry on Vance's gaunt face. The man still wore his head bandage, of course, and

Thunder knew he suffered much more pain that he allowed to show. 'Aye, I treat myself to some refreshment that I make myself and it tends to stir certain urges in me. And I go to their camps and spend time with them. I have an estimated seventeen children in these camps, eight of which are sons. There's Washo One, Washo Five—'

He began counting them off on his large fingers and Vance interrupted. 'What happened to Washos two, three and four?'

'Ask Custer and his cursed Seventh Cavalry.'

Vance nodded, wincing as he rubbed gently at his bandage. 'Why d'you yell all the time?'

Thunder smiled. 'A habit I got into. I rode alone for years and I would bellow just for the echo – just to hear a human voice, even if it was my own. I'll try to lower the volume if you be sufferin', laddie.'

Vance shrugged. 'What kind of acceent is that?'

'Oh? You dinna recognize muh Scots? Faith an' begorrah, boyo, mebbe I should try me Irish – me dear old mither came from County Cark ... or, I have a German turn of phrase I picked up once: "Ve vill shoot many buffalo, hein? Ach, Ja!" No? You don' likee? I can do velly good laundly for velly good plice. . . ?'

Vance laughed although it caused the constant pain to worsen and shoot behind his eyes. 'You're plumb loco!'

Thunder shrugged. 'It amuses the Indians. I usually am amiable enough when I visit them to give them a sort of show. A little like my reverend father – though he was never aware that his sermons were really small shows.'

43

'I've never met anyone like you before, Thunder, and I've—' Vance cut the words abruptly, frowning.

'Yes? What were you going to say?' When Vance didn't reply he added, 'Mebbe somethin' like you've never met anyone like me before even though you've travelled far and wide? Was it a memory stirring, my friend?'

'I dunno, Thunder. The words were coming of their own accord, then just – stopped.'

'Well, it could be a good sign. Now, d'ye feel like comin' with me out to the knoll? There'll be half-a-hundred buff snortin' and pawin' over that light fall of snow we had last night so as to get to the grass before it freezes enough to lose its juices and snap off. We'll shoot lyin' prone.'

Vance said he would go and rummaged in his saddle-bag for a neckerchief. That was when he found the old pink shirt. 'Why'm I keeping this, Thunder?'

'You were wearin' it when I found you. I took the notion to keep it in case it stirred somethin' for you.'

Vance shook his head. 'I don't like pink – a woman's colour. Damned if I know why I'd wear a shirt like this.'

'See? It is a puzzle added to a puzzle and you just now found another clue: you dinna like pink, laddie!'

Wakina always tended to make light of these possibly revelatory moments and Vance realized that the man did it because his head was still giving him much pain, and fresh confusion could only compound this.

'I owe you more than I can ever repay, Thunder.'

'Who says so? You shoot me six buff today, all with heavy winter hides, and you're well on the way to

44

squarin' any debt you fancy you owe me.'

Vance did better. Using the Remington rolling-block with an expertise that came naturally so that he didn't have to pause to think about what he was doing, Vance downed ten buffalo before the small herd broke and moved on over the knoll another twenty yards.

He urinated down the long hot barrel of the Remington to cool it: using water would only freeze it in the rifling. The air was crisp and the light fall of night snow was now turning to slush. Heavier falls were on the way according to Thunder and Vance shivered in the buffalo hide cape he wore over the bandages on his torso. The bullet wounds there were healing well enough but the pain in his head was daunting at times. *And the not-knowing. . . !*

His vision blurred several times and twice he had to use two bullets to drop the target buffalo. Thunder said nothing but Vance knew he was not pleased at such wastage. Bullets were precious way out here.

Coming back to the camp after midday three days later, with the downed buffalo count rising each day, they found they had visitors.

Vance felt a wariness course through him. He was feeling better today than he had since being found by Thunder and he didn't allow alarm to dull this good feeling. He had dropped a dozen buffalo this morning and the Indians were now ripping the hides off the carcasses where they lay scattered over the plains. It was rough, stinking, bloody work, slitting around the neck, down each limb and the length of the belly. Then the neck ruff was bunched, wrapped around several times with heavy rope which was fastened to a saddlehorn. When the horse was spurred off, straining, the hide tore away, leaving a gruesome stinking carcass with gobbets of fat showing against the bloody flesh and innards – all soon to be blackened with the dozens of crows and buzzards as they swarmed down.

The three riders visiting the camp watched this and the one who was the obvious leader, lanky, bearded, gun-hung, gestured with his left hand – keeping his right close to his six-gun butt. The other two called him 'Waco'.

'Had good shootin', eh, friend?' he said, in a drawling Texas accent to Thunder.

'Just fair. And I am not yet your friend, and may well not be, ever. What want you here?'

The black-bearded man narrowed his eyes, his companions, standing hipshot, their rifles slanting casually towards the ground. But Vance recognized the stance: in a flash those guns could be up and blazing with no more than a jerk of the wrist. *How did he know that?*

'No need to be uppitty, big man,' the bearded one said, baring his teeth in a tight grin. 'Just ridin' through on our way to the Sweetwater, heard your guns thuddin' – wondered if we might cut ourselves a haunch of buffalo meat? Showin' you courtesy, you see? We are starved for meat.'

'Plenty of antelope on these plains. They make mighty fine chops done on a green stick over a fire.'

The bearded man swivelled his bleak gaze to Vance. 'What you say is true, friend, but mebbe we didn't want to waste our ammunition.' He grinned suddenly.

'Lotsa Injuns hereabouts – lots who don't work for your pard there an' take a different view of white men.'

'If you'd asked friendly-like, maybe they'd have shot you a buck antelope with their bows and arrows. Saved you lead – for whatever you have in mind.'

The bearded man tensed. 'You bein' unfriendly, mister?'

'Don't see nothing to make me any other way.'

Thunder frowned, glancing sharply at Vance, but said nothing, allowing Vance to run this. The black beard moved as the Texan nodded gently. He pointed to Vance's bare waist. 'I was you, if you aim to keep that attitude – I was you, I'd get me a six-gun . . . and wear it.'

'Good idea. How about I take yours?'

Vance took them all by surprise with his words and fast-following actions. He strode forward with swift, firm steps, punching the Texan on the right arm just above and to one side of the elbow. The man howled in sudden numbing pain and released his gun back into the holster.

In a moment it was in Vance's hand and he slammed the side of the weapon across the man's head, dropping him where he stood. The Texan was still falling when Vance whirled towards the other two, seeing their rifles coming up, hammers cocking, intentions clear.

The six-gun blasted and the man with the wide-brimmed hat and who had a v-shaped nick out of the bridge of his nose reared back, his rifle exploding as it spun from his hands.The smoking barrel of the Colt

47

covered the remaining man who dropped his rifle, thrusting his hands skyward.

'Judas! Don't shoot!'

Thunder hadn't moved and the camp Indians seemed frozen in their attitudes as they crouched over the hides spread around them. Vance kicked the rifles away from the downed man and the other. The one on the ground was hugging his right arm which had been broken by the bullet. He sobbed in pain, his face slowly hardening with cold hatred.

'You ain't got much of a future, mister!' he rasped but Vance, though keeping an eye on him, ignored the threat. He jerked the gun barrel at the other man who still had his hands up in the air.

'You and your pards ride out. I don't see all three of you going over that knoll in ten minutes, we're coming after you – and we won't have to worry about getting very close. These buffalo guns have a range of over a mile and you already know we're both top shots.'

While Vance took the gunbelt and holster from the man he had gunwhipped and the other tied a neckerchief about his pard's arm, Thunder reloaded the Sharps Big-Fifty, the Sharps carbine and the Remington rolling-block that Vance had used. The gunwhipped man was coming around slowly, rubbing his head, looking sick.

'I'll know you again, mister!' he growled to Vance. 'Both of you!'

'I wouldn't think of coming back here in the hope of getting yourselves a pile of hides on the cheap, *friend*,' Thunder spoke in his bellowing voice and the trio winced. The wounded man jumped when the old hunter lifted the Big-Fifty and covered them. 'Ever seen what a ball from one of these can do to a man? My, oh, my! It is really somethin', believe me. I mean, think about how it tears a buffalo's guts to pieces, shatters that big, thudding heart like a slingshot missile hitting a crystal goble. Ah! I see you have enough imagination to know what I'm sayin'. So fare thee well, pilgrims! We'll not meet again, I think.'

The bearded man glared at Vance and savagely shook off the helping hand his companion offered. The wounded man was already sagging in his saddle, nursing his broken arm.

They rode out without looking back and Vance and Thunder watched them make good time and top out on the knoll well before the ten minutes were up.

'You not only know a lot about the working of guns, pilgrim, but you know damn well how to *use* them. What made you suspicious of those riders?'

'You mean you weren't suspicious?'

'Oh, yes, I had 'em picked as hide thieves immediately, a certain . . . air . . . about them. But you – with your brain in turmoil – you didn't hesitate to use violence.'

Vance shrugged. 'Seemed the right thing to do. You told me to follow my instincts when something stirred in my head – so I did.' He grinned ruefully. 'Hope I didn't overdo it!'

The old hunter bellowed his laugh, relaxing the tensed Indians enough for them to turn back to work, some talking in low voices amongst themselves, looking first at the now empty knoll, then back to Vance who was buckling the six-gun rig about his waist. He tried the holster in several positions, without satisfaction.

'Be best with the base tied down. But the leather's too soft – it'll flop when the gun's drawn. Maybe I'll make a firmer holster rig. Buffalo neck leather is good.'

'You see, Vance? You are well-versed in weaponry. I showed you the sheath inside your right boot for a hideout knife, and the other for a derringer? I'm afraid you have been – or still are – a man of violence, pilgrim.'

'That bother you?'

Thunder hesitated. 'In some men it would,' he said slowly. 'But you – there be somethin' about you, my friend, that keeps me at ease. . . .'

'You work on instinct, too, huh? Well, let's hope you're right – for both our sakes.'

The giant turned, lowering his head – maybe to hide a little uncertainty on his face.

Deputy Warren knew he was a dead man. He was shivering fit to rattle the fillings in his teeth but he reckoned it wasn't just the cold of this snowdrift high on the slopes of the mountain peak.

He didn't like to admit that it might be fear, but there was a good chance it was. Or maybe just the fact that he had already been hit twice by outlaw lead and he was low on ammunition: that was enough to shake up any man.

His hat was crushed on the ground beside him and, lank hair hanging across his sweat-beaded forehead, he peeked slowly around the edge of the boulder that sheltered him. Instantly a rifle boomed upslope and his face stung with rock chips. His eye on that side was gritty now, watering, blurring his vision. *What the hell else was going to go wrong?*

He shouldn't even be here! It was just that he had picked up information he wasn't even looking for and, being a friend of Bronco Madigan's and beholden to the missing marshal for one time pulling him out of a bad jam, about the worst he had ever been in before or since, he figured he was obliged to follow through.

Now look what the good deed had got him! The prospect of dying here on a freezing slope, picked off at leisure by the two or three sons of bitches up there settled in on the high ground . . . *'Man needs his head read!'*

He checked the loads in his six-gun – five in the cylinder. Then he checked his belt loops and wished he hadn't. *Only three spare cartridges. . . .*

They opened up, raking his boulder and, a man with nigh on twenty years' experience as a marshal behind him, Warren felt the knotting of his guts. *Two* would be shooting, making him keep his head down, while the third worked around to a position where he could pick him off.

Still almost prone, his wounds bleeding and hurting, he rolled half onto his side to search the slopes to his right. If the killer used the natural cover – and he would – then it was going to be a helluva long shot for a six-gun. But the man would have a rifle and that put just one more nail in Warren's coffin.

When the volley of shots sounded over there to the

right, he flopped all the way down, clawing at the earth, trying to dig himself in. But there was no hail of lead thudding into his body, or ripping up the earth, ricocheting from the boulder. Slack-jawed he raised his head, saw a man's riddled body rolling down the slope. He knew from the ragged green jacket it was one of the outlaw gang. He twisted painfully, grunting as there was a flurry of movement up there at timber-line.

A tall man with corduroy jacket flaps flying was leap-ing and sliding down towards the ledge where the other two killers waited. As Warren watched, the men there exposed themselves as they wrenched around when small rocks and dollops of snow spilled around them, dislodged by the man coming down on top of them.

'Judas priest!' Warren hissed, and a little hope of living through this after all surged through him.

That tall ranny up there, still carried down and forward by his own impetus, started shooting with his carbine butt rammed against his hip, working lever and trigger in a blur. One of the killers jerked to his feet as if someone had yanked a rope around his shoulders. He arched back over his protecting rock and yet another bullet took him in the head. There was a spout of red mist and pieces of white bone spun away in several directions.

The tall man was now on the ledge, down on hands and knees. Warren saw him roll onto his back, kick the remaining killer in the kneecap as the man fired his rifle. The bullet drove into the ground. Then the other man rose, slammed his rifle butt across the killer's shoulder, likely breaking it for the man screamed in pain. He might have saved himself if he had stayed put, but full of terror now, he staggered upright, stumbled and went over the edge. He bounced five yards from where Warren lay and the marshal distinctly heard bones break before the body slid on down, limp and lifeless.

Vision still blurred, Warren turned to look up the slope where his rescuer was now sliding towards him. He couldn't make him out clearly, but he thought, 'God almighty, only one man I know could've tackled them three that way. If I believed in ghosts I-I'd say it was Bronco Madigan!'

But it wasn't Bronco Madigan who knelt beside him to examine his wounds: it was Madigan's sidekick.

'Hell, Bronco taught you well, Kimble! I'm glad to say!'

'You need a sawbones, Gabe,' Kimble told the older marshal. 'That one in the chest is nasty, beyond my expertise. I think I can stop the bleeding on the other, though.'

Warren lay there, going in and out of consciousness as Kimble administered first aid. The young marshal sat back looking mildly satisfied.

'I think that'll hold till I can get you to a doctor. It might be a rough ride down out of these hills.'

'I-I can take it. The hell you doin' here anyway? Last I heard you was freezin' your ass in Wisconsin.'

'I've been looking for you. Actually looking for Madigan, but I came down to see you and the trail led to Fiddler's Creek where, for the cost of a few drinks, I learned you'd had a long conversation with a man called Billy Carpenter. . . .'

Warren was surprised but nodded slowly. 'Slick Carpenter's brother, a miserable back-shootin' killer. Billy was kinda upset because Slick's been killed: he says Bronco Madigan done it.'

Kimble tensed. 'I didn't know that.'

'Yeah, well, I mean Billy was barely able to talk so's you could unnerstand him, he was that drunk, but he said it happened somewhere in the Red Canyon country.'

Kimble frowned. 'That's – near the Tetons, isn't it? What the hell would Bronco be doing up *there?* Parminter and everyone else thought he was still somewhere in north Colorado – that's where he last contacted head office.'

'That's where I seen him. Billy was pretty far gone, like I said, but he was sobbin' like a kid, real cut-up, so I knew Slick was dead, all right. But whether it was Madigan killed him or not, I dunno. . . .'

He paused gasping, and Kimble gave him water from the canteen. Warren stared up at his rescuer.

'Gawd, I'm hurtin' Beau—'

'I'm hoping you'll be up to it, Gabe, but I want to get on Bronco's trail as quickly as possible.'

Warren, eyes full of hurt, struggling to stay with what was left of his life, gasped, 'Too late to worry, Beau. Billy ain't got guts enough to go after Bronco but he-he says he ain't the only one after Madigan. Reckoned Bronco killed one of the Dukes gang in a shoot-out. The Old Man, Colorado, an' young Mace Dukes, real maniac killer, was goin' after Madigan, so nothin' could save him . . . nothin'!'

CHAPTER 5

SOUTH TO
THE SUN

There were two things Vance didn't like about Fort
Fremont: the town was too damn crowded and it was
freezing.

Old Thunder's squaws had taken time off from
scraping, stretching and salting the hides to make him
a buckskin overshirt and a hip-length fur jacket. He
was much warmer than he had been when shooting
buffalo out on the plains with the old hunter, but this
town seemed to have found a direct pipeline to the
Arctic and was blasted by numbing winds and heavy
falls of snow. And his head hurt constantly.

The last few miles in with the overloaded hide
wagons had been sheer hell, worse than the previous
four slogging days. The teams were bogged – the
wheels were down over the hubs – the hides, heavily
weighted with fallen snow, tilted and spilled off wagon
number one. Number two carried less of a load and

fared better. But it had to be offloaded to free it from the drift, then was used to tow the first wagon out of the snow, afterwards being laboriously reloaded.

This happened twice in a mile and a half and Vance had had enough by the time they passed through the army's camp just outside of town. The streets were slushy, the store windows fogged over, boardwalks slippery with mud and people falling or sliding every few steps. The only good thing about it was that the hide-buyer's yard was empty of other wagons.

'Dunno how you got through, Thunder,' the buyer greeted them, wrapped literally to the eyes in furs and old rags. Even then he kept stamping his feet and rubbing gloved hands together. 'But you got the yard to yourself. Pinto McClay lost his wagonful off a cliff and I ain't had word from Whiskey Jack Larson, but there's news of renegade bucks on the loose in his country – an' he never did treat Injuns right. So . . .' – he gestured with his bulky gloved hands – 'you have a wide-open market.'

'We could be lucky, then,' spoke up Thunder. 'Hides in short supply an' here we are with two wagonloads.'

The buyer tugged at one ear lobe, barely exposed to the snapping cold. 'We-ell, might be more'n I can handle. . . .'

'If they're in short supply, how can't you handle 'em?' said Vance shortly.

The buyer looked at him with narrowed, watery eyes showing above the kerchief wrapped about the lower half of his face. 'I dunno you, feller, and you dunno the hide business. When I say more'n I can handle, I mean mebbe I don't have the cash to pay for so many.'

'But if Thunder drops his price you'll somehow manage, eh?' Vance said cynically, disgust showing.

'Vance, me an' Fanshaw here are used to dickerin',' Thunder said, with a grin that crackled the ice in his beard. 'It's traditional to kick the price around some – usually over some hot-poker rum by a warm fire, eh, Fanny?'

The buyer's eyes crinkled so maybe he smiled behind the kerchief mask. 'Fire's ready and the rum'll be buttered and spiced by the time we get someone unloadin' them hides, Thunder.' He jerked his head at Vance. 'Got a man lookin' out for you this time, huh?'

'A good man, Fanny, shot the left eye out of an eagle ridin' the thermals and the other one before the bird hit the ground. Now let's get to that fire. . . .'

Even the warmth of the fire and glow of hot-buttered rum in his belly along with a plate of food hadn't changed Vance's mind. Rubbing his temples and trying not to scowl, he waited out the long joshing conversation between Thunder and Fanshaw – they hadn't seen each other all season – and when they finally settled on a price, good or bad, it meant nothing to Vance, they shook hands and the buyer went to arrange unloading and to inspect the hides.

Vance said quietly, 'Guess I'll be moving on, Thunder.'

The old man swung up his great head so fast he jerked his hand holding his glass and spilled rum over his fingers. He sucked them dry before saying, 'Was thinkin' you could be seein' the army sawbones while you're here.'

'Why? He some kinda miracle worker?'

'He's a pretty good medic, pilgrim, and . . . I'd like to see you remember. A man needs memories. They're all that'll keep him goin' at times. . . .' He sounded wistful.

'I can't stand this cold any longer. I come from warmer climes and my blood is too thin for—'

'You know that, do ye, pilgrim?' Thunder said quickly, leaning forward to stare into the other's battered, frost-pinched face. 'You recollect you come from a warmer climate. . . ?'

It stopped Vance, for a moment. He smiled crookedly. 'One of those times when something like that just comes out, I guess. But my body tells me I need warmer weather – and that means going south. Why don't you come along? You'll get good money here and hunting's over till spring.'

'Ah, well, pilgrim, y'see I have certain interests and obligations, even, hereabouts. Some ladies to see and children to take gifts too. But I'll miss you, Vance. And I hope you find your true name. I won't try to talk you around, 'cause I can see you're sufferin' with this cold. But you'll go with full pockets. You've earned your share.'

Vance said abruptly, 'You owe me nothing. I'm the one owes you and I'm a long ways from squaring my debt.'

He jumped – and so did several other drinkers in the smoky, noisy saloon as the hunter's fist smashed onto the table, upsetting the clay jug of rum and their glasses. Luckily the jug was almost empty.

'You have earned a share of those hides, pilgrim! Argue not with me or we'll have a fallin'-out you *will* remember for the rest of your days!'

Vance smiled crookedly. 'Wouldn't change the debt I owe you one bit.'

'Aw, you be more stubborn than I allowed! Look, I did no more for you than I'd've done for anyone I found in your circumstances – and I'd hope some-one'd do the same for me. You've worked damn hard for me, freezin' your ass off, never complainin', while you're sufferin' hell with that head of yours. Now try not to tell me different! I'm a man who pays *his* debts, too. You'll take your share, or you'll be needin' a sawbones for more than a lousy memory!'

Vance laughed and finally agreed to see the doctor while Thunder and Fanshaw haggled over the final price of the hides.

The medic, named Kingsley, was a sober man, younger than Vance expected – about his own age. He sat back after thoughtfully examining the wounds and questioning Vance.

'The body wounds are healing well, and that body of yours has taken extreme punishment over the years, Mr Vance. Care to elucidate?'

'You know I can't do that, doc.' Vance touched his head.

'Mmmm.' He seemed reluctant to leave the subject of all the scars on Vance's lean, iron-hard body. 'There's nothing I can do about your memory, Mr Vance. That's a deep scalp wound, depressing a sliver of bone. May even have raised a blood clot there. It hasn't quite healed so I'd advise you do nothing too strenuous for some weeks yet.'

'You expecting me to do something violent, doc?'

'A man with that many scars, several old bullet and knife wounds among them, is not a man who sits quietly reading a book, Mr Vance. But that's your business. If you wish, I can give you the names of two very good medical men, one in Boston, the other in Washington, who just may be able to help—' He frowned suddenly. 'Why did you tense when I mentioned Washington?'

'Did I? I've got no hankering to go under the knife, especially if someone's gonna poke around in what I use for a brain. Old Thunder's pulled me out of my depression and I-I feel better. I'll get my memory back in time, won't I?'

'I'm not very conversant with such things, but I would hope so. It may be a long chance, you under-stand. . . ? Do you have any flashes of past memories?'

Vance looked at him sharply. 'I-I dunno. I *think* of some strange things sometimes. They just pop outa nowhere.'

'Tell me what kind of things.'

Vance shrugged, plainly embarrassed. 'People – faces I don't recognize. Sometimes I hear gunfire and I've had a flash of myself standing in a pall of gunsmoke, gun in hand. Twice I saw what I was shoot-ing at: a man in a livery stable that I shot and he fell through a window; and a – robber, I think, near a stagecoach with blurred people standing around while he held some young feller in front of him . . .' He paused and it seemed to the doctor that his eyes were

60

haunted when he said very quietly, 'I shot the young *hombre*, in the head . . . not the robber. Now why would I do that. . . ?'

The doctor remained silent, looking thoughtful as Vance dressed, and tugged on his gloves, nodded briefly. 'Doc, I'm obliged. But surgery ain't for me. Hell, I cringe when I need to go to the dentist. Guess I'm just too yellow.'

The army medic smiled. 'A man carrying all those scars could never be called *yellow*, Mr Vance.'

'Thunder insists on paying your bill. That OK?'

The medic waved it aside, shook hands and watched Vance hurry out into the cold. He understood the man's . . . reluctance to face such major surgery, but it was disappointing . . . even one chance in a hundred was worth taking.

In the end, Vance capitulated and accepted a hundred dollars from Thunder, although the old hunter wanted to give him more. 'This'll see me way down south to some sunshine, Thunder. It's more than enough. You've given me that claybank as well as all the supplies I need. You say I've earned it, but in my book I'm still beholden to you and always will be. You ever need help of any kind' – unconsciously brushed his right hand against the six-gun he wore under the flap of his fur jacket – 'you send for me. I'll let you know where I'll be.'

Thunder knew it was no idle promise and he shook hands firmly, holding the grip as he looked down into Vance's rugged face. 'Been an honour knowin' ye, pilgrim.'

'And knowing you, Thunder. You're a queer Joe,

but you've got a heart big as a bull buffalo. I'll never forget you.' He smiled ruefully. 'Mebbe I'm the queer Joe, saying that when I can't even remember my own name.'

Thunder snorted. 'You take care – ride far and fare thee well, man-with-no-name.'

'*Adios*, Thunder.'

'See? Another Spanish word. Mebbe you should travel as far south as Texas?'

'I might do so – somewhere warm, anyway.'

He rode off without any further delay and the old hunter stood in the spitting snow and biting wind, watching him ride slowly away from Fort Fremont, wondering what the future could hold for a man like Vance with no memory older than a few weeks.

Deputy Marshal Gabe Warren was wounded more seri-ously than Kimble thought. He drifted into a coma and died on the second day after the marshal brought him in.

There were legal matters to be settled with the local law, Sheriff Barnaby O'Dowd. He was a leather-tough man, dried-out looking, wore a permanent stubble tinged with grey and hadn't been known to smile in the three years he had enforced the law in Fiddler's Creek.

'Well, that about settles the paperwork . . . too bad you didn't get here a mite sooner, Marshal.'

Kimble stiffened, feeling his face tighten into hard lines. 'Why d'you say that?'

'Warren wanted to move on, follow-up on some-thin', but he said he'd wait around a day or two, see if

there was a message from Washington, or someone
turned up to lend him a hand.'

'He'd finished his assignment.'

'So he thought, too, but there was a wire, told him
to sniff around, see what he could find out about this
missin' feller. Then he hunted-up Billy Carpenter
again, kinda spooked him, I think. Billy ran and
Warren followed.' He shrugged bony shoulders. 'Ran
into Billy an' his pards, I guess. Pretty game goin' it
alone, you ask me.'

'No one did ask you, Sheriff.'

O'Dowd arched his eyebrows. 'Tetchy, ain't you?'

Kimble sighed. 'Yes, I am – Sorry. Everywhere I go I
get told I'm dragging my feet.'

'Well, when fellers get killed, you know how it is.'

'Unfortunately, yes, I do. Now, Gabe was talking
about some place called Red Canyon – you know it?'

'Know of it – long ways from here. Across the
Tetons. I can show you a map and a trail but I hear tell
that in real life that trail'd stop a chim-pan-zee dead in
his tracks.'

'People make it across,' Kimble said shortly. 'I'll
outfit and try my luck – meanwhile I have to telegraph
my boss in Washington.'

The sheriff took him to the door and pointed out
the telegraph office at the end of the street near the
rail depot. Kimble thanked him and, as he was leaving,
the sheriff said, 'Billy Carpenter got a wire tellin' him
about his brother – operator might be able to tell you
where it come from. If that'll be any help.'

'It will be. Obliged, Sheriff.'

Kimble hurried down the street, self-anger building. *Why the hell hadn't he thought of that!*

He was really starting to worry about Madigan now: all along he had kept telling himself that Madigan was OK. The man was a maverick, a law unto himself when on assignment or at any other time that suited him. But time was passing now without any word or sightings and winter was here – and one of Madigan's pet hates was cold wind and snow.

He would endure them, though, if he had to, in order to finish his assignment. That was what made Madigan such a good marshal: he would endure anything, risk his life, go up against impossible odds, and as long as he was breathing, he would complete the job.

He had tried to teach Kimble a similar outlook and Beau thought he'd been a pretty good pupil, but so far he hadn't done much more than get annoyed because folk kept telling him he wasn't moving fast enough. He recalled once, Madigan saying, straight from the shoulder as usual,

'*You're too self-centred, Beau. You've got the makings of a good marshal, but you get mad too easy about things that don't matter, or things you can't change. Try knocking that chip off your shoulder when you get told you ain't measuring-up, or you've made a mistake. Learn from these things, don't lose sleep stewing about 'em. In case you ain't figured out what I'm saying, Beau, here it is, straight: grow up.*'

That seemed a long time ago and he thought he was shaping-up OK. Madigan didn't pull his punches though, and he set mighty high standards.

But Kimble knew this much: he *would* find Madigan. Dead or alive.

The town was called Trinity and nestled in the north-western corner of Trinity Basin, giving a fine view of the Sangre de Cristo Mountains and the distant northern arm of a meandering river.

The mountains deflected the northern winds and protected the basin from the icy cold. He had felt the difference in air temperature as soon as he'd ridden through the Raton Pass. The basin was watered by a high tributary of the Canadian River and the town looked prosperous.

There were fertile farms on the way in and the rise of lush green slopes were dotted here and there with the red and black of cattle. Something seemed to click in his midriff and he knew this town attracted him. Already he had shed the heavy buffalo jacket and tied it behind the claybank's saddle. Texas might be warmer but this was – welcoming.

There was a short wooden bridge over Trinity Creek at the edge of town and many of the buildings and some of the houses were adobe, common clapboard structures scattered amongst them.There was a small plaza in the town centre.

Stabling the claybank and leaving his gear at a rooming house by the creek where he booked in, Vance walked out into the sunshine, under cloudless blue skies. Sure different to Fort Fremont.

The place was busy, plenty of traffic, wagons, buck-boards, a couple of fringed surreys and folk on the walks looked happy enough. He searched for a saloon, saw one on the south corner of the plaza. Crossing a side street, he heard a rough voice down an alley.

'You been warned, *señorita*! Don't put up no more bob-wire fences or Mr Kelso ain't gonna be so polite next time. You savvy what I'm sayin'?'

Vance saw them then. Two men who looked like cowboys crowding a small young woman in fringed riding skirt and checked blouse against the adobe wall of a storehouse behind a freight depot. Her hat was awry on her dishevelled black hair, which seemed thick and profuse.

The woman was struggling, looked like a Mexican. She kicked the big blond man holding one of her shoulders against the adobe and he lifted a meaty hand threateningly. The other stood by grinning, saw Vance, and the grin faded.

'The hell you starin' at, drifter? This is Flyin' K business. Keep movin'.'

'Sure,' Vance said, and kept moving – straight down the alley with long, purposeful strides, taking the cowpuncher by surprse.

'Tully!' the smaller cowboy said urgently, gesturing to Vance.

The blond man turned as his raised arm was suddenly gripped powerfully, yanked back, pulling him off balance. He jerked the woman with him, had to release her as Vance spun him around. He didn't speak, just drove a fist into the middle of the man's rugged, startled face. Tully grunted, staggered against the wall. The girl ducked and swung a quirt dangling from her left wrist as the other cowpuncher started to rush in. It took him across the neck and he grabbed at the place as he broke stride. The woman kicked him

66

hard in the shins and the man howled, dancing on one leg.

Vance met Tully as the man came at him, nose bleeding and upper lip split. His fists were big and Vance dodged two driving blows, but caught one on the left ear that made his head ring. His skull was already aching and the hot blood flashed through him. He braced himself, caught the next blow on a forearm, jerked upwards abruptly. He drove his left fist three times rapidly into Tully's face. The man had nowhere to go as the adobe wall was at his back. Vance crowded him, threw a right, hammered his chest and midriff. As Tully's legs buckled and he doubled over, Vance lifted a knee, crushing him back against the wall, head hitting hard. Tully dropped to his knees and the girl cried, '*Watch out!*'

Vance spun but the cowpuncher had made a comeback, thrust the girl aside roughly and slammed hard into Vance, knocking him off balance. The cowboy swung gloved fists in hard, hammering blows, without much aim, but connecting well enough. Vance's head buzzed and throbbed and it drove him into a relentless fury.

The cowpoke jumped back, but Vance grabbed the front of his jacket and crouched as he swung the man full-tilt into the wall. The cowboy shuddered and gagged and Vance drove him back again, let him fall as the girl cried out something.

The blond Tully shoved her aside with enough force to send her tumbling, and his right hand started to lift his six-gun. Vance was two steps away, closed the gap in a fraction of a second and gunwhipped Tully to his knees, his Colt barrel blurring as it battered the man's head and face, streaking it with blood and torn flesh.

Tully was finished before he stretched out on the alley floor with the accumulated rubbish. The cowboy was huddled against the wall, face in the dirt, breathing like a blacksmith's bellows.

'Quick! This way! There are other Flying K men in town!'

She tugged his arm and led him down the alley and out into an area behind the freight yard, along a narrow path edging the creek and into a yard over-grown with weeds. She took him to a rear door in a small building and pushed him inside. The place smelled musty and was cluttered with boxes.

'We will be all right here.' She was a little breathless and he could smell a sage-like perfume coming from her. It was dim, the room some kind of storage place, and he could just make out her small face and the glisten of her eyes. '*Muchas gracias, señor!* I try not to use Spanish so much in town, but it seems to suit best at this moment. I am *very* grateful.'

'That's OK, *señorita*,' Vance said, settling his breathing, Colt back in holster by now. 'They rough you up much?'

'Not much. They were more . . . threatening. They think they can frighten me.'

He felt himself smiling. 'They didn't succeed.'

Cloth rustled as she shrugged. 'It is not the first time. Sooner or later Kelso will resort to violence.' She paused and added, hesitantly, 'Perhaps – soon.'

'Because I beat-up a couple of his crew? Well, I

didn't see any other way.'

'You could have kept walking.'

'Not after I seen them bullying you.'

Her teeth flashed in a smile and he was surprised to feel her small hand on his a forearm. 'You are the kind of man I am looking for: would you like to work for me?'

CHAPTER 6

'BET YOUR LIFE'

Her name was Merida Alvarez and her ancestors had ranched the entire Trinity Basin a hundred years earlier. They had died one by one in an epidemic of influenza, a few fleeing east where the survivors of the family eked out a living, too young or too old, too ill, or suddenly too poor to return to the land opened up by their forefathers when the Spanish empire stretched this far north of the Rio Grande.

After the epidemic had passed and by the time the survivors had recovered their health, Trinity Basin had already been settled by *Anglos*. The territory administration of that time refused to recognize the old Spanish Grants that went back all the way to Coronado and the *conquistadors*. It took almost twenty years for Merida's father, the last of the bloodline leading directly back to the original *hidalgos*, to fight for his heritage through the courts. It was very complicated and the strain eventually killed him. Some folk resented Mexicans wanting to oust them from land

70

they had developed for themselves during that time. Their outrage was heard all the way to Washington, and the US courts saw no reason to dislodge American settlers who had built up their own town and thriving community. In fact it was seen as political suicide to even contemplate such a move when progress of a new town was advancing satisfactorily in an area where population and stability were badly needed.

But as Merida was the last of her family, except for Rico, a younger brother who had not yet reached his majority, the law made a compromise, under some mild pressure from Mexico City who wished to tread lightly in their relationship with the *Estados Unidos* for the present.

The original deed for the Alvarez family was for 23,000 acres, much of which now was occupied by various ranches and businesses and people, including Nathan Kelso and his large Flying K cattle ranch. But there was still almost 250 acres with a creek frontage and forest belt unused in the south-west corner of Kelso's holdings. He had no use for the land although the water was good, but it would take too much clearing to make grazing pastures when he had sufficient already to hand. He was approached by the territorial governor to allow Merida to use the land – it would help keep relations with Mexico City on an even keel. In exchange, Kelso would enjoy certain tax concessions which he found hard to pass up.

Still, he did not relinquish his hold gracefully, but in the end, he agreed to Merida being deeded the 250 acres. It was part of her family's original land and, although it wasn't what she had wanted, she was smart

enough to know it was this or nothing. So she determined to put her energies and resources into making
it into a viable spread. There was even a possibility she
could expand into the foothills at a future date. But
her brother, Rico, was lazy, haughty, as if he was the
original *hidalgo,* and gave her little help, but lots of
worry. She hired hands to clear some of the forest and
a lot of it was completed. But Nathan Kelso had been
simmering all this time about having land he regarded
as rightfully his taken away from him. And, he made it
known, he didn't care for Mexicans as neighbours.

Kelso's kin, far south and long ago in Old Texas,
had been run off land they had tried to grab by force
from the Mexican *hidalgos* who at that time administered enough of Texas to earn it the title of 'empire'.
There had been a lot of blood spilled – much of it
Kelso. And Nathan was a man who could not forget.

So Merida's men were beaten and frightened off.
She refused to bow to Kelso's pressure, but the local
law, Sheriff Dade McLintock, a friend of Nathan
Kelso's, made it mighty hard for her. Still, she refused
to be intimidated.

She told Vance all this passionately as they rode
back to the ranch, three hours from town, at a
leisurely pace. He had accepted her offer to work for
her as a cowhand.

'There will be much work with horses,' she told
him.

'That's OK – I'm pretty good with horses.' The
words spilled from his lips but he had no idea why. *Was
he good with horses or was he just saying that to get the job?*

'Good, then welcome to A-Star.' She looked mildly

72

embarrassed. 'I like the star symbol and I hope one day I will turn this land into an A-grade ranch. An "Alvarez" Star.'

'Worth a try,' he allowed as they came at last to the turn-off from the main trail. 'I can see the creek and where you've been clearing the trees. If you blast the biggest stumps you shouldn't need to fell many more.'

Merida looked at him sharply. 'You have a good eye for the needs of a growing ranch, Señor Vance.'

'Just "Vance".'

She nodded. 'It is your first or last name?'

'Does for both.' He saw her frown and hesitate as if she was about to speak, then change her mind and ride on a little ahead. 'You can see the house from this knoll.'

It was a mix of log and adobe, with a sod roof, the grass standing upright in dark-green tufts. It blended in well with the brush behind and the creek at the foot of the rise. He saw a well in the front yard and silently approved. She was obviously intent on staying put. The corrals had a permanent look to them as did the small barn and stables. There were cows in the distant pastures.

'How long have you been here, Merida?'

'Just over a year.'

'You've done well.'

'I – think so.' Her voice flattened a little. 'But the money is dwindling and Rico's wasteful lifestyle does not help.'

Vance didn't remark on that. 'How many men've you got working for you besides me?'

'I have only one now. Kelso has frightened some

away. My ranch hand is named Mitch Hanlon. He knows his work, but sometimes does what he wants to, not as I tell him . . . I think he resents taking orders from a woman.'

And a Mexican one at that, Vance thought but remained silent as they rode on down into the small yard.

Rico wasn't home, wouldn't be for a few days: he was staying in town with 'friends' so Mitch Hanlon told them, eyeing Vance suspiciously. He was a flabby, middle-aged cowpoke, had a slyness about him, as he looked at the girl.

'I take orders from him? Or he takes 'em from me?'

Merida looked at both men. 'You both take orders from me.'

That didn't seem to please Hanlon and in the small bunkhouse later, watching Vance unpack his meagre belongings, he said, 'I been here three months. I got things goin' the way I like 'em right now. Don't you do nothin' to foul it up.'

Vance flicked his eyes towards the man briefly, went on unpacking.

'You hear?'

'Not anything that interests me.'

Hanlon stiffened, stood up from where he had been lounging on his bunk. 'Listen, drifter, you got that fiddle-footed look to you. Don't think you can come in here, stir things up, then get itchy feet and move on and leave me to start all over again – you better savvy that. Don't think because I'm older I can't take care of myself!'

'As long as you get it easy like you've been making it.'

74

'What's that mean?' Hanlon bristled, head thrust forward belligerently. He dropped a hand to his six-gun butt – then went white and stepped back, gasping for breath as Vance straightened, holding his own Colt, cocked, in his hand. 'Whoa! Jesus, man – I never even seen you draw! Why-why din' you say you were a hired gun? Hell, I ain't in your class. OK, OK! I guess she's hired you because of Kelso and told you what she wants done – you go ahead an' do it! I-I won't give you no trouble.'

'I know that, Mitch.' Vance had not yet lowered the hammer, or the gun itself.

Hanlon licked his rubbery lips, breathing raggedly. 'She mighta told me, though! I been wonderin' when she'd get around to hirin' a gunslinger. But you better be good, mister! Kelso and his crew ain't no bunch of Sunday-school kids!'

'You been beat-up yet?'

Mitch seemed embarrassed.'They cornered me in town one time. Tully an' that sidekick of his, Ferris.' He licked his lips. 'They hit me a couple times in the belly an'-'an' said they knew I wasn't gonna give no trouble, so just do my chores as long as it didn't affect Flyin' K and I'd be all right.'

Vance nodded. *Tully would have recognized that Mitch presented no danger.*

'They don't think much of me, I guess, but they can be mean. Nigh killed one of the ranch hands one time. Scared Rico. He don't spend much time here, since.'

'Thanks for the background, Mitch.' Vance slid the gun back into its holster.

Hanlon, relieved, swaggered slightly. 'That's OK, Vance. Anythin' I can help you with, anythin' at all. . . .'

In the end, Kimble hired a man on Sheriff O'Dowd's recommendation to take him through the Tetons to Red Canyon. He was glad he had when he saw the extent of the place from a ridge whipped by icy winds, high against the grey skies.

'My God! What a tangle,' he exclaimed, and the guide, name of Geary, sniffed hard, spat and wiped his moist nostrils on the sleeve of his patched woollen jacket. He envied Kimble his Canadian-made wool-and-fur hip-length coat.

'Injun renegades hide out in here – some white outlaws, too.' He had a twisted face, this Geary, and squinted one eye when he talked. 'You tell me what you're lookin' for and might be I can help. This is my bailiwick.'

Kimble studied the man briefly. Geary didn't know he was a US marshal and he didn't aim to tell him. 'Friend of mine was last heard of in the general area. I've put a few things together and played a hunch, based on what I know of his character, and I think he came through here on the trail of someone.'

Geary was leery now. 'He law?'

'Sometimes takes a badge when he's short of cash,' Kimble said vaguely. 'But this feller he wanted was with others. Maybe a man called Slick Carpenter. . . .'

Geary grinned, showing mostly leathery gums. 'Uh-huh. Think I get the idea . . . not all legit huh?' He held up a gnarled hand wrapped around with rags for

warmth in lieu of gloves as Kimble made to speak. 'It's
OK. Told you this is my bailiwick. I got friends among
the Injuns: they keep me posted. . . . Slick coulda been
here. Say, your friend happen to be partial to pink
shirts?'

Kimble blinked. 'Not as far as I know.'

'Well, I dunno the details but I heard there was a
shoot-out in the canyon – few weeks back, little longer.
Feller in a pink shirt shot his way outa one ambush,
but rode into another right after.' He tugged at one
earlobe. 'Now here's where it gets kinda strange.'

'In what way?'

'Well, there's two things coulda happened
accordin' to my Injun friends. . . .'

Kimble waited when Geary stopped speaking. And
waited. Finally he frowned and snapped impatiently,
'Well, *what* for God's sake?'

'Two things—'

'You already said that! You—' Then Kimble
tumbled and he nodded jerkily, angry at himself for
not realizing right away the man wanted more money.
'How much?'

'How good a friend was he?'

'*Was* he?'

Geary grinned. 'Slip of the lip. How about a couple
hundred?'

'Two hundred what? You're surely not talking two
hundred *dollars!*'

'Ain't I now? Listen, friend, I can just ride off and
leave you to find your own way out, which you'll never
do. You might draw your gun and tell me to take you
outa here but I could take you lots of places where *I'd*

get out but you wouldn't – b'lieve me, coupla hundred bucks is cheap.'

Kimble was fighting down his temper now. Unfortunately, he knew Geary was right. 'I can give you fifty now but I'll have to owe you the rest. I'll write an IOU that the bank in Fiddler's Creek will honour.'

'Knew you was a reasonable man. Ta, my friend.' Geary pocketed the coins Kimble handed over, folded his hands on the saddlehorn. 'Two things I was told about a feller in a pink shirt: he killed Slick Carpenter, which is pretty damn good, but was shot in a second ambush.' He studied Kimble's reaction: deep frown. White-knuckling the reins, trying to control the shock on his face. 'T'other, was that an old buffalo hunter took him away. Alive or dead is anybody's guess.'

'There buffalo around here?' Kimble asked, sceptically. 'I thought they favoured plains country?'

'Sure, more to the north. But this big feller was chasin' one that was already wounded – mebbe he done it an' wanted to put it outa its misery.' He spat. 'Damned if I'd ride through the Tetons to do that for any dumb animal.'

'Forget your finer urges for now, Geary. Who told you these two things? And how reliable is the information?'

Geary gestured vaguely at the hills. 'Injuns. Can't trust none of 'em, and one lot'd been on the fire-water—'

'Which you supplied?'

Geary shrugged. 'Can take you to see 'em if you want to find your man bad enough.'

Kimble wondered if it was all lies, a trick to get him

deep into these hills where he could be murdered, robbed of what money he had and his equipment and clothing, both of which were far superior to anything he had seen around Fiddler's Creek – or out here.

But if that man in the pink shirt had been Madigan – and he had no real reason to think it might have been – could he take the chance of not believing anything Geary had said?

'How far?' he asked abruptly, and Geary spat again before grinning widely.

'All the way there an' back, friend!'

'Glad to hear you say "and back",' Kimble said, suddenly producing a six-gun. That wiped the gummy smile right off Geary's face. 'Because this gun will be pointed at you all the way, Geary. If I don't come back, I'll guarantee you don't, either.' He smiled coldly at the worried-looking guide, 'In fact, you can bet your life on it!'

CHAPTER 7

NORTH TO GUNSMOKE

There was lots of smoke. Bitter, reeking, throat-rasping powdersmoke that ripped at a man's lungs and eyes. The noise! God almighty, it was like standing within a clap of thunder – a hundred *claps of thunder!*

Cannon were roaring endlessly, the barrels beginning to glow red hot. One exploded as the soldiers tried to ram a fresh load home too soon, shredding the crew. Above this deafening pandemonium there rose another sound, a different kind of roar, from hundreds of throats, raging blood in the veins exploding in this insane clamour as men in grey and ragged clothing surged up the slope into the very mouths of the cannon, line after line dropping as if a scythe had swept their ranks, stepping on and over their comrades' bloody bodies. The long knives of the bayonets stabbed into the blue iniforms of the defenders, pistols cracked, rifle butts smashed flesh, broke bones – and he felt the slice of a Yankee bayonet in his side and screamed in pain. . . .

'Goddle mighty! What in hell's goin' on. . . ?'

The rough hand shaking his shoulder and the fright in the voice that filled the small bunkhouse brought Vance jerking out of his nightmare, drenched with sweat. He blinked and stared up into Mitch Hanlon's startled face, a lamp turned low on the table. Vance sat up slowly, lifting a finger to indicate he was all right. He held his head in both hands, rocking gently. His skull felt split wide open.

'Man! I thought you was goin' plumb crazy! You were screamin' somethin' awful. "Roundtop"! Yeah That's it.' Hanlon looked more closely, now. The sheet had fallen to Vance's waist and he saw scars on his torso and part of the man's back that was closest. 'You fought at Gettysburg?'

Vance blinked. 'What? What's that. . . ?'

'Judas! *Gettysburg! Little Round Top!* A butcher's shop, I heard. I was in a different part of the war.' He didn't elaborate and suddenly Vance nodded, using the corner of the sheet to wipe his face.

'Yeah – old nightmare. Shakes a man up.'

'Sure damn well shook me up!' Mitch squinted. 'You been havin' a few lately. T'other night you yelled, clear as you talkin' to me now – "I had to shoot him somewhere an' his back made the best target!" An' not long after, you said, "Hell, Joe – or Bo, somethin' like that, I need you like a bullet in the head!" ' He wilted a little under Vance's steady, unnerving stare. 'I – din' say nothin', figured it weren't my business.'

'No, but I dunno what it was about,' Vance said truthfully enough. 'Thanks for waking me, Mitch.' He was still holding his head, rubbing gently at both temples.

Mitch gestured. 'You do that a lot – rub your head that way. You got problems? Old war wound or somethin'? I mean, you got that many scars—'

'All that was long ago, Mitch,' Vance said without conviction. Mitch believed the 'long ago' part OK, but the man looked and sounded as if he *wasn't sure*. Mighty strange.

Vance smoked, sitting on the stoop of the bunkhouse for a while: he had done a lot of that, alone in the night with his scrambled thoughts. But, come breakfast he seemed almost his old self, a little pale and drawn. When Merida asked him if he would break-in two particular horses from the bunch of mustangs he had trapped recently, he looked uneasy.

She added, 'I want to give one to Rico – he has always liked horses and caring for it might help his interest in A-Star.'

'Maybe I might leave that for a day or two, Merida.'

She frowned, fresh and energetic as usual, her dark eyes studying his face. 'Is everything all right, Vance? You look a little poorly this morning.'

'I'm fine,' he said shortly, and she swung her gaze to Mitch who blurted, 'He's been havin' nightmares! About shootin' men in the back and fightin' bloody battles on Little Round Top.'

'Shut up, Mitch!' Vance said it mildly enough but with a whipcrack undertone and Hanlon closed his mouth abruptly. Merida looked tense. 'I-I get 'em occasionally. Hasn't happened for a long time. Gives me a bad headache. That's why I'd rather leave the bronc-busting for now, Merida.'

'Ye-es, all right, Vance. There are plenty of other

chores to be done.'

But his unease didn't go away and he knew he would be watched a lot more closely now. He didn't want to have to tell her his memory was blank – and he knew these nightmares somehow must be connected to the disturbance in his brain. He didn't want sympathy and he didn't want to lose this job. He felt – comfortable here: it was a strange but welcome feeling.

He had enjoyed the last couple of weeks setting burlap-and-brush blinds to trap mustangs, sorting the animals, bringing in the best to the ranch corrals, fighting them every inch of the way, doing homely chores. He felt at home here. And that eased his confusion and edginess.

He was helping Mitch make a new barn door when Merida brought him a telegraph message in a yellow envelope.

'Rico brought this back from town. He is upset. Said he was confronted by Tully and Ferris demanding to know when you're going to town next.' Her eyes searched his face, 'I think perhaps they remember the night you rescued me.'

He nodded. 'Their type don't forget that kinda thing easy.' He ripped open the envelope, read briefly, then looked up. 'Merida, hate to do this, but I'll have to drag my time.'

She looked puzzled and Mitch said gruffly, 'He means he's quittin'.' There was no trace of sorrow in his voice.

Vance ignored the man, waved the paper. 'A very good friend of mine has been hurt and he's got some trouble. I'm beholden to him so I have to go. Sorry to let you down, but I really do have to help him.'

He could see she wasn't happy, but she surprised him by saying, 'Of course – I understand. I am willing to keep the job for you, Vance. You are an excellent worker and you know so much about horses – which, as you know by now, interest me more than running cattle on my ranch.'

He moved from one foot to the other. 'Likely to be gone a few weeks.' She started at that. 'Got to go up to Wyoming, and when I get there, might be I'll have some more trailing to do.'

'But if your friend is injured and in hospital, won't you find him easily? I mean, you wouldn't have to search. . . .'

Her words drifted off as she saw his set face and he spoke quietly, 'I said he has troubles. He can't do anything about them while he's laid up: I can.'

Mitch whistled softly through his blubbery lips but no one took any notice. 'Must be some kinda friend!'

'I understand a man's loyalty to his friends,' Merida said slowly. 'It is part of the old *hidalgo* way and it is an admirable thing, but – forgive me, Vance – you do not look very well this morning and there have been other days. . . . Would you be up to such a self-imposed duty?'

'I owe it to him, Merida,' he said simply.

Mitch shook his head slowly: it was beyond his comprehension. But the girl understood. 'You go and help your friend, Vance; come back when you have finished. And your job will be waiting for you – if you wish to come back, of course. . . ?'

'Yeah, I do, Merida, and I'm much obliged.'

'What about Tully and Ferris?' Mitch said suddenly, looking apprehensive. 'If they're on the prod and you ain't around they'll pick on me!'

Vance set his bleak eyes on the man. 'Don't worry about Tully and Ferris,' he said flatly. 'They won't bother you.'

He didn't have to go looking for the hardcases.

Tully and Ferris must have been watching Merida's A-Star ranch and when he reached the fork in the trail, about halfway to town, the Flying K men rode out from behind some boulders and blocked his progress. Ferris held a carbine in his lap, finger on the trigger, thumb on the hammer.

Tully's face hadn't yet healed completely and from five yards away Vance could see the bruises and scabbed cuts and grazes. He kept riding in slowly, left hand holding the reins, right resting on his thigh near the six-gun's holster.

'Far enough, drifter!' called Tully in his rough voice, but Vance kept riding. He didn't use the spurs or reins to increase the horse's pace, just walked it on towards the two men. 'I said "far enough"!' Tully sounded edgy now.

Vance kept his horse moving towards them. It disconcerted them both, even more so when he suddenly halted and said, 'Step aside, gents, I've business in town.'

'You got business *here!*' growled Tully and at a jerk of his head, Ferris raised the carbine threateningly, thumb still on the hammer's ear.

Vance nodded. 'OK, let's get it over with. You want to kick my butt because of the alley, right?'

It was coming a little too fast for both men and Tully frowned, Ferris willing to follow the big man's lead. 'Or did Nate Kelso tell you to run me out?'

Tully curled a thick lip, a half-healed split showing, the lip itself still swollen and purple-bruised. 'Oh, you'll be out of it, all right, Vance! Boss has left it to us what we do, and seein' as the sheriff is kinda – attached – to Flyin' K, I don't think we need stop short of puttin' you outa commission permanent! *Ferris!*'

He yelled his pard's name loudly, possibly in some way hoping to distract Vance, and reached for his own gun.

Vance shot Ferris first, seeing as he had a weapon already in his hands, and the man grunted as he was slammed back over his mount's rump. He was still falling when Vance swung his Colt towards Tully whose gun was just clearing leather. The man's eyes grew larger, doubled their size practically, and there was a split-second's hesitation, but he kept the gun coming, swinging it forward and up into the firing position.

Vance shot him out of the saddle, too, just one bullet as it had been with Ferris.

Both men were dead when he examined them. He draped them over their mounts and took them into town. A crowd followed him down Main to where he stopped at the hitch rail outside the law office. Someone had already alerted Dade McLintock and the sheriff was standing hipshot on the small landing outside the door, a sawn-off shotgun in his hand. He was tall, trim, mid-thirties, and smelled of pomade or hair tonic. His clean-shaven jaw jutted like a granite ledge in the Sangre de Cristos.

'I'll have your gun, cowboy,' he said conversationally.

'Not today, Sheriff. This was self-defence. I don't have witnesses so you'll have to take my word.'

'Why should I do that? You're a known trouble-maker. You made enemies of those men the moment you hit town.'

'Well, I guess it's up to you, but both have been shot once apiece, with my six-gun. They stopped me on the trail in from A-Star. Ferris already had a rifle in his hands. Carbine to be exact.'

Watching Vance closely and suspiciously, the sheriff spoke to a man at the front of the crowd. 'Take a look at their guns, Zeb, 'specially Ferris's carbine.'

The townsman did so and announced, 'Neither one been fired, Sheriff.'

'That's right,' Vance said. 'I outdrew 'em both.'

'You said Ferris was holding a cocked carbine on you . . . You must be *mighty* fast, drifter!' That brought a snigger from the crowd as Dade looked around for approval.

'I said Ferris was *holding* a carbine. He didn't cock it – or tried to – till Tully went for his own gun.'

There was a total silence except for town sounds on the street. All eyes were on Vance.

'You're saying you beat the fall of Ferris's gun hammer?' The scepticism in McLintock's voice was very obvious and the crowd were with him there.

'Yeah, I guess I am. You want to cock that shotgun, I'll show you how.'

87

The crowd murmured again and now all eyes were on the lawman. Dade McLintock's eyes were narrowed. 'I think this town'd be better off without you, Vance! I aim to look into this proper. Now you lift your hands and I'll lock you up till I've done just that. . . .'

'Until you get your orders from Kelso, you mean?'

The sheriff's anger got the best of him and he cocked a hammer and started to swing the shotgun, but stopped the action instantly.

He was looking down the barrel of Vance's Colt, rock-steady, hammer spur back under his thumb, trigger already depressed. Even if the lawman somehow managed to shoot Vance, the six-gun would still fire – and McLintock was right smack in line with the barrel.

'I'm on my way north, Sheriff,' Vance told the man easily. 'A friend of mine's in trouble up that way. I've brought in two men I killed while defending myself. I've made my statement in front of all these witnesses. Now, here're the dead men and I'm moving on. Is that all right with you?'

McLintock glared, big jaw trembling in suppressed fury, eyes slitted with hate.

Vance started backing-up the horse and the crowd opened out. No one tried to stop him and, of his own accord, the sheriff laid the shotgun – uncocked now – on the landing at his feet. He didn't raise his hands but he kept them away from his holstered six-gun as Vance turned and put the spurs to his claybank.

A week later he arrived in Fort Fremont and learned Old Thunder was in the army hospital. The same doctor who had seen him before was waiting.

'Thanks for sending that wire, Doc,' Vance said.

'Thunder told me you'd sent word you were working in Trinity Basin. Are you managing all right?'

'I'm managing. What happened, and how is he?'

'He's seriously injured, but I believe he'll pull through. Never seen a tougher man of his age. He was robbed. Jumped along the trail as he made his way towards the Indian villages with a burro laden with gifts for his wives and children. . . . Someone shot him in the back. There were at least two, possibly three, it seems. They took everything, including his clothes, left him naked and bleeding in the snow. I still don't know how he didn't freeze.'

'But he's gonna be OK?' Vance wanted to make sure.

'We have to watch he doesn't develop pneumonia, but the wound's healing. Yes, I think I can say he'll get better – eventually.'

'Know who did it?'

The doctor studied Vance carefully. 'I believe there was some kind of information wired in here by a sheriff from Trinity who claims you shot and killed two men there.'

'They were trying to kill me.'

'Seems the sheriff's none too sure. He wants you apprehended and sent back – in manacles.' Vance waited. The doctor frowned. 'That doesn't seem to bother you.'

'Not what I'm interested in right now, Doc. Who backshot Thunder and robbed him? That's what I want to know.'

The medic looked hard at Vance. 'I wouldn't shave off that beard around here. You were clean-shaven when you were here last. And I don't think you should see Thunder, or someone's going to put the pieces together and realize you're the man McLintock wants arrested.'

'All right, Doc, all right! I'll take your advice, but for hell's sake tell me who did it!'

'Unfortunately Thunder didn't see them clearly. He was knocked unconscious by the bullet. When he came to, he was naked, freezing, and alone. But he does remember, just as he was coming around, hearing a voice giving orders to leave him and ride out. He said it was a Texas accent he'd heard before, a man with a black beard. He mentioned a name but it was slurred. I think it was Waco.'

Vance nodded gently. 'Know who he means, Doc. Thanks. I'll head on out if you'll tell me where it happened.'

'I can do better than that. There are three men who've been hanging around town, spending big – at least two of the three are Texans, according to my source, and the other might be from Kentucky. Has a deep scar across the bridge of his nose. And one of the Texans wears a black beard.'

Vance smiled. 'Doc, I could almost kiss you. No, no! You're safe, but I'm mighty pleased. Where's this trio holed up?'

The medic hesitated. 'All hell will cut loose if you try anything here!' Vance waited impatiently and the medic sighed. 'They have a cabin at Sagehen Creek, to the west. Not exactly a full-blown goldfield but some gold has been found and there's quite a sizeable prospectors' camp. This trio claim that's where they're getting their money. They trade a little gold occasionally but some say they rob the successful miners. No proof, though.'

'Doc, I won't forget this—'

'Says the man who can't recall his own name!' The medic smiled and waved a hand. 'Sorry! I was just being a smart-mouth. You haven't remembered, have you?'

'No, Doc, and don't worry about the wisecrack. I've been having strange dreams, though. Maybe I'll find time to tell you about 'em.'

Vance skirted the fort and the town area and went into the brush as he made his way to the prospecting area: as the medic said, it was too small yet to be called a goldfield. It was late afternoon and he waited until sundown before riding in amongst the scattered tents under a light fall of snow.

Bearded, dirty men appeared, some holding rifles or shotguns, a few with guns in hand, all with firearms close by, letting this stranger know they were ready if he had any notions of trying to jump their claims. Vance nodded affably enough to one man standing with a mug of coffee in his gnarled hand. 'Step down and have you a cup of Java, friend.'

'Believe I will. *Gracias, amigo.*'

Vance let his claybank's reins trail, accepted the cup of hot coffee the man poured from a blackened tin pot.

'Here to try your luck?' the man asked, and Vance

knew this was just a news-seeking interlude.

'Not for gold,' he said, and saw the interest start to fade almost immediately in the other's lined face. 'Looking for three men – coupla Texans, maybe, and a Kentuckian, or maybe he's from Tennessee.'

'Couple of "mebbes" in there, friend. Sounds like you dunno these gents any too well.'

Vance sipped, said nothing, watching the man over the rim of the mug. The miner pursed weathered lips, gestured to the mug in Vance's hand. 'Finish your coffee. Sorry I cain't offer you any vittles.'

Vance smiled crookedly. 'Nicest way I've been told to move along in a coon's age. *Amigo*, this trio are not friends of mine, nor are they friends of an old man who's now in the infirmary with a bullet in his back and empty pockets. I'm here to see those three about that.'

The man squinted for a long moment, slurped some of his own java. 'There's a cabin across the gulch where you see them droopin' pines. Was half-burned once, been repaired with some logs and clapboards. Rough job. The three rannies you want stay there. Mean bastards, I hear.'

'Obliged, *amigo*.'

As he mounted, the miner said quietly, 'I heard about Ol' Thunder. He gonna be all right?'

'Doc says so.' He lifted a hand as he rode off, the oldster squinting after him.

A small camp-fire outside the shack, amongst puddles of slushy snow, had burned down some and was untended. There was a smell of burned food on the air mingling with the woodsmoke, the clatter of cutlery and murmur of voices inside.

Vance had his rifle, shell in the breech, thumb on the hammer spur, ready to cock. It was full dark now which suited him and he stood from his crouch beneath the snow-laden branches of a fir tree and shivered. It was a hell of a lot warmer down in Trinity Basin. Quicker he got this chore done, the sooner he could get back there.

'*Hoped* it might be you, you son of a bitch! Been kinda expectin' you since we nailed that old bastard of a buff hunter! An' I ain't forgot that gunwhippin'!'

A gun muzzle bruised Vance's spine through the heavy fur jacket and he froze, recognizing that Texan voice. 'And I was hoping you'd be with the others, Waco, you back-shooting scum.'

That last was just to rile the killer and it did – more than Vance had intended. He felt the gun muzzle withdraw and instantly knew the man was reversing his hold to knock him out with the rifle's butt. Vance dropped, spun onto his back, rammed his Winchester upwards and felt the muzzle sink into the killer's midriff as he triggered.

The shot was muffled. The blast blew Waco back a couple of feet. The man dropped to his knees, screaming with the pain – but not for long. Vance shot him again and by that time the other two in the shack were shooting at him.

He shoulder-rolled over the fallen Waco, slid down the slushy slope away from the feeble light of the dying camp-fire, bullets ripping into the ground around him. He spun about on his belly, levering in a fresh shell, triggered at a gunflash inside the partly open doorway. Wood splinters tore loose, a man cursed. Vance kept rolling. Three fast shots ripped up the ground where he'd sprawled a moment ago.

He was down in a hollow now, saw that it ran parallel to the cabin. Crouching, breath beating in the back of his throat, he ran along there. Guns in the shack still sought him near where Waco lay. He climbed the slope, came up on the same level as the ramshackle building, made out the flimsy rear door leading to the path to the privy.

He didn't hesitate. Just lowered his shoulder and ran, hitting the door like a charging bull, wood splintering and tearing loose. He went in, stumbling, rolling, sliding. The two men crouching near the front door, spun about wildly, one falling on his side. The other reared up, bringing his gun around and Vance braced himself, worked lever and trigger, sent the man spinning out into the dark yard with three fast shots hammering him into a rag doll. He dropped the rifle – it must be empty now although he hadn't been counting his shots: he didn't aim to risk trying to finish the fight and find he had only one bullet left in the magazine.

The surviving killer was outside now and running. Vance tripped over something on the floor, picked himself up, heard a horse whinny. The man came riding out of the shadows under the trees, lashing with the rein ends, the other hand holding a gun, shooting wildly at the cabin.

Vance dropped to one knee, chopped his left hand at the gun hammer. It roared and bucked and the rider hurtled from the saddle, crashed to the ground, rolled several feet and flopped onto his belly.

Head ringing and feeling off-balance and groggy now from his exertions, Vance climbed to his feet by holding the edge of the splintered door, smoking gun hanging down at his side. He leaned there heavily, waiting. . . .

By the time he felt up to reloading his weapons, an army patrol had arrived and he lifted his hands out from his sides as their guns swung to cover him.

The sweating sergeant rode in closer, army-issue Remington revolver covering Vance.

'Mister, you might just have done us a favour, cleanin' out this rat's nest, but you better hope one of 'em's alive so's we can get some kind of story to compare with whatever lies you think up to tell us!'

Oh-oh, Vance thought.

CHAPTER 8

MADIGAN'S WAY

Colonel Farraday was a no-nonsense career army officer, sporting a Custer beard and hair cropped close to his head, mostly metallic grey. His eyes looked tired, but agate-hard, as he read the statement Vance had been ordered to write.

'Be better if you were some kind of lawman, Vance,' the officer said eventually. He waved the two hand written pages. 'This is vigilante stuff – not acceptable – officially.'

'Figured I did you a favour, Colonel.'

The colonel frowned. 'You did someone a favour – those men've been a thorn in my side for a long time but they had everyone up at Sagehen Creek scared white, afraid to talk out against them. Now that's all the "thanks" you can expect from me.'

'Getting rid of those three is the same as cleaning out a rattler's nest, no thanks necessary.'

The officer stared long and hard at Vance and the man in manacles did not look away. 'Well, the trouble is that the goldfields are just beyond any legal jurisdiction and therefore beyond army law ... but let's move along. Doc Kingsley told me about your association with that old buffalo hunter and your – what d'you call it – affliction?'

'A goddamn nuisance, Colonel, is what I call it. Not comfortable when you dunno who you are.'

The officer grunted briefly. 'I cannot even begin to imagine. But, Vance, you're a man who knows how to use a gun and from all reports you use it with deadly proficiency. You see where this leads my thoughts?'

Vance nodded, tight-lipped. 'Sure, I could be a gunfighter or bounty hunter ... or outlaw.'

'You shot to kill, but with reason, I guess. That Tennesseean lived long enough to admit to the goldfields' thefts and robbing your buffalo hunting friend. Whatever you are, you have a damned ruthless streak.'

Vance tried to spread his hands, forgetting for the moment they were manacled. 'Take your pick, Colonel. I can't help you.'

The colonel pursed his lips, stroked his little pointed beard thoughtfully. He sighed. 'Somehow, I believe that so I'm not taking the shooting of those three killers any further. However, I have an official request from Sheriff McLintock to apprehend you and I'm duty-bound to do it. Have already done it. I can't release you. You'll have to go back to Trinity in chains, I'm afraid.'

'Damn it, Colonel! Those men down there waylaid me, meant to kill me. It was self-defence.'

'You lack a witness to back your story, though.'

'Yeah – well, I can see it's no use arguing with you,

but can I at least talk with Ol' Thunder before I leave?'

'Provided Doc Kingsley agrees. I'll be sending a non-commissioned officer with you as escort to Trinity. But I warn you, I will choose one of my most experienced men. You make trouble along the way, Vance, and you'll surely find it. Any favour you might've done me no longer counts. But – that gunfight will show on my report as a quarrel between three greedy thieves and claim-jumpers . . . a dispute over ill-gotten gains.'

Vance knew he couldn't hope for more and that was sufficient. He was lucky the colonel had taken such a liberal view. . . .

Shortly after he was in the infirmary speaking with Ol' Thunder, a soldier standing guard at the door.

'You got . . . trouble,' the old man said, indicating the manacles.

'Little, down in Trinity – I'll be OK. You look more chipper than I expected.' Vance was lying of course. The old man looked terrible. The bullet wound had taken much out of him and lying for so long, naked in the snow, had done him no good at all. As if to confirm this, Thunder coughed rackingly, wiped his mouth with a grey, blood-spotted rag.

'Caught up with those Texans and got your poke and some cash and gold nuggets from their shack. Colonel's gonna sort it out, so you'll get most of your money back.'

'A little too late, pilgrim, but I thank'ee.' He was wheezing now and one big, gnarled hand with all the scars and blotches from long years in the wilderness, reached and tugged at Vance's hand. 'Might not get to see my wives . . . an' brood now. They won't let 'em come to me, of course.'

'Doc Kingsley says you'll be OK.'

'He says!' Thunder coughed hard again and he seemed to collapse in on himself. Vance wished he had had time to spend with those murderous sons of bitches before he put a bullet in them . . . they'd have left this life screaming!

Hell! What kind of man does that make me? he asked himself.

He forced a smile and held up his cuffed hands. 'Gotta wear 'em all the way back to Trinity – and the sheriff there ain't on my side.'

'You makin' a life for yourself down there, pilgrim?'

Vance thought about that: it was something he hadn't considered. But the fact was . . . Before he knew what he was doing he was telling Thunder about Merida and the A-Star and Flying K, unaware how enthusiastic he sounded.

His huge wheezing filling the room, the old buffalo man nodded when Vance had finished, one of those claws of hands lifting a little. 'Stay down there, Vance. It seems uncommon . . . good. The woman, too. . . .'

Vance started. 'I just work for her, Thunder!'

'Your voice gives you away, pilgrim! Despite all, I detect a touch of happiness.' He tried to chuckle but it changed to a coughing bout and left him barely able to talk.

Kingsley must have heard and came in, frowning, moving quickly to the old man and sounding his big, though bony chest, his eyes on Vance. He rolled them towards the door and Vance got the message, stood slowly. The soldier straightened too, alert.

'Guess I better be going, Thunder. They want to put me on the stage in Sweetwater – start of a long trail.'

The old man knew he hadn't long. 'Doc, there's a poke of money due me accordin' to Vance. You take half an' I'll tell you which reservation and who to send it to. The rest – you make Vance take it. Hush, pilgrim! I-I ain't got the strength to argue. You've earned it. If – if you need a lawyer or somethin' down in Trinity, it might . . . help.'

Doc Kingsley frowned and shook his head at Vance, begging him not to get the old man stirred-up. 'Thunder, I'll always be in your debt. *Muchas gracias.* And *hasta la vista!*'

'You're a damn Texan, you know! Figured it all along.' Thunder said, showing a little of his gums as he stretched his leathery lips in a half-smile. 'Well, s'pose there has to be some good ones amongst all them tall streaks of misery.' He managed a cackle without choking.

Vance took the bundle of bones that was Thunder's right hand and squeezed briefly. 'I'll let you know when I find out who I am. If ever.'

Thunder managed another chuckle without coughing but the soldier looked as if he thought Vance was loco, talking that way. 'Stay as you are, pilgrim . . . stay. . . .'

When he eventually arrived back in Trinity, there was a wire waiting from Dr Kingsley.

Ol' Thunder had gone to his Happy Hunting Grounds even before Vance and his escort had boarded the stage at Sweetwater.

Merida was allowed to visit him in his cell behind

McLintock's law office, but the sheriff stood with folded arms in the passage doorway all the time. He looked bleak and unbending, ears cocked.

She told Vance Kelso had come to A-Star after Tully and Ferris were killed and accused her of deliberately hiring a gunfighter. She didn't know if she had convinced him otherwise.

'He came again when he heard you were coming back to be locked up,' she added. 'This time he was gloating, telling me that now I only had Mitch Hanlon to work for me and that I would find it very hard to hire anyone else. So it would be wiser for me to leave – he offered me a ridiculously low price for A-Star.'

'You tell him where to put it?'

She seemed nervous. 'I stalled. I do need funds, Vance – I may have to accept. Kelso also approached Rico who promised he would try to persuade me to sell and leave.'

'Rico got authority to do that? He's not yet twenty-one, is he?'

Hesitantly, her mouth tightening, she nodded. 'I put the ranch in both our names. I thought if Rico had something he could call his own, some . . . asset . . . he might take an interest and help me build up the ranch.'

Vance had only seen Rico a few times: he was a waster, figured the world – including his sister – owed him a living. He would always take the easy way out, and profit where he could and never get his hands dirty.

'I guess I'm not going to be much help in here, Merida. McLintock is supposed to be investigating,

101

but I don't see him straining himself, and I suspect Kelso has told him to lock me up and throw away the key.'

'You watch your mouth, drifter!' the sheriff snapped from the doorway, listening. 'You're in enough trouble already.'

'You cannot hold him!' Merida said curtly. 'All the evidence points to Vance's story being true! No court would even entertain a prosecution for murder!'

McLintock smiled thinly. 'Now, I wouldn't be so sure, *señorita*. Mr Kelso has friends in the legal profession and he's consulting with them. He's entitled to justice after all, it was his men your man killed—'

'In self-defence!' she said sharply.

'Well, now, that's what we gotta find out, ain't it? I'm in no hurry. I aim to do a thorough job on this.'

'In other words, Merida, Kelso's told him to keep me locked up till you decide to sell,' Vance said, and the sheriff scowled.

'I think you've visited long enough, Miss Alvarez. You're upsetting the prisoner.' He pointed a stiffened finger at Vance. 'And you shut your mouth! You got too damn much to say!'

Merida looked at Vance quickly, and he smiled thinly. 'Thanks for coming, Merida. You want any money to help out, I've got some coming from Old Thunder. It'll be transferred to the Trinity Bank from Fort Fremont in the next week or so. You take what you need. I'll arrange access for you.'

'Oh, no, Vance! I couldn't! You must use it to hire a lawyer. I will see to it, if you like—'

'I told you the visit's over!' McLintock said, grabbing the girl's arm and half-carrying her out of the passage kicking the door closed behind him.

Vance stared at that door between the bars he held with his hands, knuckles white.

How the hell could a man have so many different troubles land in his lap in so short a time?

Beaumont T. Kimble paid Geary the remainder of the man's fee he had charged to take Kimble to see the Lakota Indians who lived in the hills.

The tribe had been expecting Ol' Thunder, but he hadn't yet arrived and the Indians were obviously worried, had sent a man to search for him. They knew little about the man in the pink shirt, but thought he might still be alive. Ol' Thunder was the man to ask about that.

Then, just as the white men were leaving, Kimble bitterly disappointed that his lead had fizzled out, a messenger rode in with news that galvanized the Indians.

Geary said, 'Ol' Thunder's dead. Died from a bullet in the back. But, get this: some feller the doc sent word to showed up, went after the three *hombres* they reckoned had robbed Ol' Thunder, and killed 'em all in a wild shoot-out.'

Kimble stiffened. 'Who is this man?'

'Dunno. Some friend of Thunder's, beholden to him, I reckon, to go after them three hardcases alone like that.'

'By God! That's Madigan's way!' Kimble said, eyes sparking. 'Did you say "beholden" to the buffalo hunter?'

'I said he might've been. I dunno. Just guessin' . . .'
Geary paused, snapped his fingers. 'Judas! Could be
the feller in the pink shirt! Squarin' away with
Thunder.'

'Let's get down to this Fort Fremont!' Kimble
snapped, turning his mount even as he spoke.

Geary had earned his money in Kimble's opinion,
but it was a pity they were too late to talk with Ol'
Thunder.

They found his fresh grave on Boot Hill, separate
from the army cemetery within the stockade of the
fort. Geary left Kimble, went off to find the sutler's
store to spend some of his money. Kimble sought out
Colonel Farraday and identified himself.

'We could use regular visits from US Marshals out
here,' the colonel told Kimble, handing back the identification papers. 'This fuzzy edge of army-civilian
jurisdiction is one big pain in the ass. Makes for far too
much paperwork. Half the time the outlaws' light-out
before we get the go-ahead and we're left with egg on
our face.'

'I'll put it in my report to the chief marhsal,' Kimble
said, stalling easily. *Something he had learnt from Madigan
who was a man who would do and say almost anything as
long as it enabled him to finish his assignment properly.* 'Too
bad I didn't get to talk with the old man, but what can
you tell me about this feller who shot it out with the
trio on the goldfields?'

'Vance? Now, there's a strange one, Deputy Kimble.
My God, he's tough and he certainly is proficient with
guns! And not short of courage! If I'd had enough
evidence, I'd have sent a squad of men after those

three killers long ago, but your Vance . . .' He paused and shook his head, not without some admiration. 'He went in there like a one-man stampede, they tell me. Killed two on the spot and the third died later, after admitting to the crimes. . . . He seems decent enough understand, but there's a look about him. I heard some of my men call him "Lean 'n' mean". I like "ruthless": he seems a man who's determined to see the job through at any cost, take any risks. . . .'

'Can you describe him?' Kimble tried to keep his voice firm and casual. But so far, this sounded mighty like Bronco Madigan! In actions, if not physical appearance.

'He had a beard, full-face one, but I don't think he wears it all the time. About as tall as you, perhaps a little taller. Lean as a rail, face gaunt from what I could tell behind his beard. Doc Kingsley treated him when Thunder first brought him in and he tells me the man's body is covered in scars. . . .'

Kimble leaned forward quickly, startling the officer. 'Scars? Old bullet and arrowhead wounds? Others that could've been made by a whip?'

'Good God! Deputy, you'll have to ask the sawbones for details. D'you know this man Vance?'

Kimble on his feet now, impatient, said, 'I believe I do, Colonel, but his name's not Vance. Now where can I find this doctor of yours?'

Milton, the senior clerk jumped almost a foot in the air when he heard the clang of the bell through the door of Chief Marshal Parminter's office summoning him. But what really got him moving fast, under the amused stares of the the other more junior clerks, was the chief's voice bellowing, 'Clerrrrrrrk!'

The fact that Parminter didn't even use his name told Milton that the chief marshal was not in a good mood.

When he opened the door and saw the living thundercloud behind the big desk, the clerk swallowed, notepad ready. 'You wanted me, Marshal?'

'I didn't make all that racket just to make sure you were awake! What news is there?'

'Sir, I have sent telegraph messages to places ranging from the Canadian Border down to the Rio Grande—'

'Goddamnit! Never mind about trying to cover your back! What word is there from Kimble?'

A pause and then, 'None, I'm afraid.'

He expected an enormous explosion but strangely, Parminter's face straightened and he shook his head slowly. 'I hope to hell I haven't got another marshal missing!'

'We had that sighting from Deputy Magill. He thought he saw Kimble near the rail depot in Cheyenne.'

Parminter waved the words away. 'I don't want *possible* sightings. I need a message in black and white! What the hell does Kimble think he's doing?'

'You – er – did tell him to go wherever he felt he had to, sir, and do whatever was necessary to locate Marshal Madigan.'

Parminter glared and the clerk seemed to wilt. 'All right, Milt. Send more wires, as many as necessary! But, dammit, find Kimble now! I've got marshals wandering all over the damn country, my two best men missing, and still no sign of Johnny True! Or what the devil he's up to!'

It was the paytrain for the mines out at Flying Duck sprawling in the foothills of the Otero Range. Biggest paying mine in the territory, it employed almost 200 men and they were paid monthly, the lucky ones off-duty going back with the empty special train to the bright lights of Castle Creek. With overtime and extra shifts, the payroll was enormous and was guarded by a dozen armed men.

The train rounded the bend, coming to the trestle bridge over the Castle Creek gorge, fifty feet high above the narrow muddy stream and rocks below. The engineer was at his ease as they approached, slowing a little for the last bend, enjoying the breeze at the cab window. The cowcatcher of the locomotive had just reached the beginning of the bridge when there was an explosion that rang through the foothills, gouts of dirt and stones hurled high, together with uprooted bushes – and the heaving loco, its front end twisted and mangled.

The engineer had time to straighten up, his hand closing over the brake as he yelled at his assistant. Then the bottom literally dropped out of his world.

With a certain amount of grace, the loco sagged to one side, a mass of twisted metal in front now, its weight dragging the tender and the three still moving special cars over the edge, wrenching the rails from their ties.

There were men in those cars: armed guards,

accountants for handling the complicated pay-out, the traditional train guard in the caboose. The screeching sounds of the dying train and the remnants of the explosion drowned out their cries and in seconds there was only a pile of splintered wood and distorted axles below, one heavy wheel breaking loose and carving a deep trail down to the water's edge. Smoke and steam and flames roared and hissed. The caboose had torn loose, rolled over and over to land upside down, walls collapsing, ten yards from the main wreckage.

A band of men came out of the trees and more appeared on the far side on the steep slope. These latter were afoot, holding rifles and shotguns. None was masked and the leader was a gangling youth with a pimply face, his bone structure seeming to want to break through the acned skin.

Whistling slightly between his buck teeth he wandered through the wreckage and, when a bloody body twitched or moaned in its last throes, he didn't hesitate to put a charge of buckshot into it.

'Find the pay-chests,' he called in a thin voice, and the tough, bearded roughnecks obeyed instantly, actually running, hurling aside the smashed timber and metal while he stood there with one boot on a jutting granite rock, forearm across his bent leg, surveying the havoc he had caused. He hawked and spat, looked up to the pale-blue sky.

'Colorado – you'd be right proud of me!'

'Here they are, Mace!' a man yelled. 'Judas! There's a leg lyin' across two of 'em!'

Mace chuckled, moving forward now. 'Well, find the owner. Otherwise he'll have to limp his way to

Hell, won't he?' He laughed louder at his own joke. 'Might even get his ass singed. Now, the rest of you drag them boxes out here, pronto!'

CHAPTER 9

US MARSHAL

Kimble had never felt so downright exhausted and beat since his training days under Bronco Madigan, a mighty hard taskmaster. Slumped way down in the saddle, he walked his hired grey gelding into Trinity, dirty, beard-stubbled, hungry and tired, tired, tired.

He had missed Doc Kingsley at Fremont – he had been called to attend wounded in some skirmish with renegades – and, impatient, instead of resting up, he had set out immediately to track down the man everyone called Vance. He had pushed himself at a killing pace on the long arduous ride, but he was here in Trinity now, barely able to sit his saddle.

Dozing in leather, he was halfway along Main before the traffic noise jarred him awake and a man on a loaded Conestoga cracked a whip close to his ear, yelling, '*Move*, you dumb bastard! You're blockin' my way.'

Kimble started awake, dropped a hand instinctively to his gun butt as he looked around a little wildly.

110

Madigan had hammered that reaction into him until he did it every time he woke from a sleep now. Even after romancing some sweet-smelling gal, his hand dropped to his bare hip, searching for his gun butt. It had been a cause of amusement many a time and once or twice it had scared the ladies into leaving pronto. They didn't like the notion of being in bed with someone who felt he had to reach for his gun, even if awakened by a gentle blowing in his ear. . . .

Now, the wagon driver sucked in a sharp breath and dropped his whip at his feet. 'Take – take it easy, mister! I never meant nothin'!'

Kimble got his bearings fast enough and irritably waved away the man who suddenly seemed happy enough to muscle the heavy Conestoga around Kimble's stationary horse.

Sheriff Dade McLintock witnessed the incident from his stoop, where he lounged against his law-office door, smoking. 'You keep that gun in leather while you're in my town, feller.'

Kimble set the gelding across to the hitch rail. He tried to stifle a yawn without success. 'Sheriff, I'm Deputy US Marshal Kimble and I understand you're holding a man I'm interested in. . . ?'

McKlintock was alert now. 'An' who might that be?'

'I believe he calls himself Vance right now.'

The sheriff smiled crookedly. 'Ah! One of them with half-a-dozen names, huh? No wonder I couldn't find a dodger on him. You look plumb tuckered, Marshal. Why don't you go get cleaned up and catch up on some sleep before you see my prisoner? He ain't goin' nowhere.'

111

Kimble was impatient to see if Vance was indeed Madigan, but he knew he wasn't at his best and took the sheriff's advice.

It was after lunch before he returned to the law office, clean-shaven, wearing fresh clothes, rested, and with a meal inside him.

'I'll need to see some identification,' Mctlintock told him and Kimble produced the necessary papers. Handing them back after scanninng, the sheriff asked, 'What's this Vance done that they send a US marshal after him?'

'What's he done that you're holding him?' countered Kimble. McLintock didn't care for this kind of sparring, but he was leery about crossing a federal man.

'Killed a couple cowpokes a few weeks back. I ain't satisfied it was self-defence like he claims.'

'Got any proof?'

McLintock hesitated, shook his head. 'Not really.'

'You have or you haven't, Sheriff – which?'

'All right, so I can't prove it wasn't self-defence, but I know damn well he had it in for those fellers.'

'And likewise? They had it in for him?'

'They'd tangled before. Aw, go and see him! You must want him bad to come all this way, so s'pose I'll have to co-operate.' He didn't sound convincing: he didn't really want to let Vance go. Kimble wondered why. . . .

McLintock led the way down the passage and when they approached the cell block, Kimble said, 'Wait in your office, Sheriff.'

'Now, hold up! This is my bailiwick and—'

'And I'm a federal marshal and I want to interview this prisoner in private. Go back to your office, McLintock.'

Dade coloured and, muttering, heeled sharply and went back, slamming the passage door after him.

Kimble was already standing at the bars of the cell and Vance, dozing on the bunk, opened his eyes at the sound of the slamming door. Kimble was just a dark shape against the early afternoon glare coming through the high, barred windows. But Kimble could see him clearly enough: the man had sure lost weight, his face narrower than ever, more like a skull than the wolf features Kimble remembered. But he moved the same, a little slower maybe, but still with that easy gait like a cat, ready for anything.

'Bronco?'

A tentative query, but he was almost certain this was Madigan, just changed some physically, maybe through illness or when recovering from a wound, or. . . .

Vance swung his legs slowly off the bunk, stood up and walked across to the barred door. He had been allowed to shave and slick back his hair and he narrowed his eyes some as he stared at the man on the other side of the bars.

'Who you looking for, friend?' Then he saw the badge on Kimble's new shirt. 'A US marshal! What the hell is McLintock playing at now?'

'It *is* you, Bronco! Come on, you know me: Beau Kimble.'

Vance went very still, looking over Kimble again, wary now. 'Got the best of me, friend – name's Vance.'

'So I hear.' Kimble lowered his voice. 'But you're really Marshal Bronco Madigan – Chief Parminter's had me looking for you for weeks. We lost contact with you and he's getting all edgy about Johnny True.'

'Johnny True? Sounds like something out of one of Ned Buntline's books!' Vance squinted again, moving closer, heart pounding hard now. 'You really think you know me?'

'Damnit, Bronco, what is this? OK, I understand you might be undercover right now but we're alone here and I have to be able to report to Parminter that you're OK and on True's trail . . . now drop the dumb act, will you?'

Vance stood closer to the bars. 'Look at this.' He bowed his head, pulling the hair aside and Kimble winced when he saw the deep, still-red scar across the man's scalp.

'By God, you're lucky you weren't killed!'

'Knocked me cold. When I came round I couldn't even remember my own name.' A pause, then, a whisper, 'Still can't.'

Kimble froze. 'Must've had concussion from a blow like that. It could affect your memory. No wonder you didn't stay in contact. I guess you still get confused. . . ?'

Vance smiled thinly. 'You could say that.'

But Kimble was too excited, more convinced than ever he had located his friend, and he missed Vance's sardonic tone. He snapped his fingers. 'You're the man in the pink shirt! I've been hearing stories about it for weeks. No one seems sure about what exactly happened except someone in a pink shirt was shot in

Red Canyon and taken away, dead or alive, by an old buffalo hunter.'

Vance watched the other's face. 'The Indians called him "Old Thunder". He's dead now.'

'Yes.' Kimble stared back levelly. 'Before he died someone showed up, tracked down the men who shot him and killed them all in a blazing shoot-out.' His eyes crinkled as he looked at Vance. 'Now that is exactly the kind of thing Bronco Madigan would do.'

Vance tensed, said tersely, 'I dunno about that, but Ol' Thunder couldn't help himself – and I owed him.'

Kimble grinned. 'See? Typical Madigan thinking!'

Vance chose to ignore the comment. 'He kept that old shirt I was wearing when he found me, smart enough to know I'd be all mixed-up after a wound like I had. Thought it might help me remember things. But I just can't figure me in that colour . . . whoever I am.'

'It might've had something to do with your assignment at the time. I've worked with you for a couple of years now, Bronco, and I've never known you to wear a pink shirt or anything else that colour – but that doesn't matter. I'm beginning to piece things together.'

'Half your luck.' Vance was tensed, head throbbing. *A US marshal! That was the last thing he would have thought of – but was it true? Could be – what would Kimble have to gain if it wasn't? But why wasn't he more excited?*

Kimble said soberly, 'You must be going through sheer hell. We'll get out of here and go back to my hotel room and talk about old times, and your assignment. Something's bound to stir and you'll recollect.'

Vance smiled thinly. 'They say pigs might fly some day, too. . . .'

'Don't think that way, Bronco!' Kimble said sharply, moving down to passage door. 'Try to remember. Try damn hard!'

Vance stayed at the bars, gripping the cool iron. He was frowning, all knotted-up inside, his head pounding now, worse than ever, forcing him to squint against the pain.

Kimble might be optimistic but nothing had stirred in Vance's memory at anything the man had said: not a single thing. He didn't even recognize *Kimble. The man was a total stranger to him in every sense – and yet, if he could positively identify him. . . !*

He didn't even know how he felt right now!

He could recall *nothing* beyond the moment he had opened his eyes in Red Canyon and found Old Thunder bending over him: not even how he came to be headshot. And the worst thing of all was that he had the overwhelming feeling that he never would remember beyond that moment. No matter what Kimble told him. For Vance, that was when his life began. . . .

McLintock was seated behind his desk and in a sour mood, having taken offence at the way Kimble had dismissed him earlier.

'I want you to release your prisoner into my custody, Sheriff,' the marshal said, entering the office.

McLintock, leaning his elbows on his desk, stared blankly at first, then began to smile slowly. 'You do, huh? An' s'posin' I don't want to release him?'

Kimble flipped his vest aside and tapped the marshal's star. 'You know the deal – federal law takes precedence over local.'

McLintock's smile tightened only slightly. 'You'll need to gimme a damn good reason why I should co-operate with you, Kimble.'

'I've just given you one, but to save all this devious head-butting, I'll give you an even stronger reason.' He leaned down and spoke almost in McLintock's face, the sheriff rearing back, startled. 'That man in there has a head wound and needs medical attention – he won't find it here.'

The sheriff frowned, blinked several times as he digested this, then gave that crooked smile again. 'So you say. Now, I'll believe you're a marshal because you've showed me papers that say so and with all the right seals and so on, but, far as I'm concerned, Vance's just a hired gun who shot down two cowboys mindin' their own business. I dunno what you're playin' at but I ain't releasin' no prisoner of mine with-out the say-so of someone a lot bigger'n you – *Marshal!*'

Kimble's eyes were bleak and he saw this made McLintock uneasy. 'McLintock, I'm going to take your prisoner with me. You want to argue, go ahead. You want me to wire Marshal Headquarters in Washington and get authority from Chief Parminter? OK – but if I was you I wouldn't count on keeping my job as sheriff if somehow the chief marshal gets the notion that some two-bit lawman in a half-baked town is doing his best to obstruct a federal investigation. . . .'

The sheriff leaned back, fingers locked behind his head as he smirked up at Kimble. But his bravado didn't come across too well for his voice shook and he began to sweat profusely. 'Now, normally I would give you a fight on this – I mean, I'm holdin' this man on a *murder* charge, not some piddlin' little thing like bein' drunk an' disorderly or brawlin'!' There was even a hint of a plea there now and Kimble could see McLintock despised himself for letting it show.

'You admitted you can't prove it wasn't self-defence.'

'Gimme time!'

Kimble straightened, face hard now: he'd had enough. The sheriff paled, tensed so that his shoulders stretched the material of his shirt.

'No! I'm giving you nothing but an order to release your prisoner into my care, Mclintock – I'll make out the necessary papers, take full responsibility. *Now!*' Dade actually jumped in his chair, taken aback by the coldness in the young marshal's voice and eyes. 'No more nonsense. Let's go get the prisoner.' His hand dropped casually to his gun butt.

McLintock stared up, breathing a little faster than normal. 'You can't come in here an' throw your weight around just 'cause you're wearin' a marshal's star!'

Kimble slapped his hand flat on the desk. It sounded like a gunshot and papers began to fall and slide. McLintock slammed back in his chair. *Kimble knew Madigan would have the man knocked slack in his chair and bleeding by now but Beau pulled up short of that. Still. . . .*

'All right, all right!' the sheriff said, standing quickly and taking a ring of keys out of his desk drawer. They clinked as his hand shook. 'Jesus! you damn feds!'

FIND MADIGAN!

*

From the office window, McLintock watched the two
marshals ride slowly out of town, after paying a brief
visit to the telegraph office. They crossed the wooden
bridge over the creek before becoming lost to sight
behind the screening cottonwoods. He reached down
his hat and adjusted it and took a rifle out of the rack,
then locked the street door before going back into the
empty cell block.

He left the building by the rear, saddled his horse
in the yard and rode out through the sagging gate in
the fence, across the shallow part of the creek. He left
town by devious trails using buildings and stands of
timber so he would not be seen.

A couple of hours this side of sundown, he rode his
sweating, hard-driven mount into the large yard of the
Flying K, watched curiously by working ranch hands.

Kelso was a big man, fat-big, and he showed his
annoyance when the sheriff burst in through the side
door of his office where he was working on some stock
sheets.

McLintock didn't waste any words or even remove
his dusty hat. He went straight to the rancher's desk,
leaning his big, sweaty hands on the edge.

'That damn greaser bitch has sent for the US
Marshals!'

The words shook Kelso. He had been allowing his
anger to boil up as he prepared to tongue-lash the
sheriff for the way he had entered. Now the lawman's
announcement stopped him dead so that he blinked,
had to swallow and change direction swiftly as he

sorted out his thoughts. 'She's what. . . ?'

'That Vance! He's really a US marshal named Madigan, workin' undercover, makin' out like he's a mustanger!'

Kelso frowned, absorbing this. 'Now, these are pretty wild accusations, Dade. If you're right – well, someone here could be in a lot of trouble!'

'Oh, I'm right!' McLintock said emphatically, pleased at the way he had caught Kelso on the hop. 'What's more, there's a second marshal named Kimble come to help Vance.'

Kelso sat back, feeling the blood drain from his face and the choking feeling rising into his throat. *Two federal marshals!* Then he pulled himself together, staring hard at the sheriff.

'Find a chair!' he snapped, not liking the way McLintock was standing over him at the desk. 'Then tell me *exactly* how you know all this, Dade – and it better be good! If you've let your imagination run away with you. . . !'

Seated now, the lawman grinned. 'I got this straight from the hoss's mouth, Nate. That Kimble son of a bitch pushed me around some, made me go wait in my office while he interviewed *my* prisoner! In *my* cell block!' He snorted. 'Dumb bastard! Never told me nothin', just hid behind that marshal's star! I let him think he got away with it.' Here, Dade McLintock looked mighty sly. 'You know that old waterpipe runs through my office to the cell block?'

'When Old Sheriff Seccombe was going to pipe water to the cells? Yeah, but as far as I know it was never connected.' Kelso smiled faintly. 'Just another "pipe dream".'

The sheriff smiled crookedly. 'Nope, never connected. Just a'sittin' there along my rear wall – behind my desk. A big, empty hollow pipe.'

'You've tapped into it, I take it, so you can listen to what's said in the cells whenever you want.'

McLintock's smile faded fast. *Damn* Kelso! The man had spoiled the whole thing. *Smart-ass!*

But he sighed and told the rancher what he had heard of the conversation between Kimble and 'Vance' by listening at the vents he had cut in the disused waterpipe.

'Real name's Bronco Madigan . . .' He felt some elation as Kelso straightened slightly and wrote the name on his notepad. 'Playin' it safe, he wouldn't even admit that to this Kimble. Might not've met him before but Kimble knew him, all right. Vance even tried to make out he'd lost his memory!'

Kelso tapped his pencil absently against a stone ink well, looking mighty thoughtful. 'Seems a bit odd.'

'I told you what I heard.' Dade bristled.

'All right. This part about a pink shirt. . . .'

'I didn't savvy that. Not important, anyway.'

'Maybe yes, maybe no. But I knew a man once who favoured pink shirts. He's dead now.' He paused. 'Killed a couple of months back, up north – by a man named Madigan.'

Chief Marshal Parminter looked up irritably from the pile of field reports he was wading through: not one contained good news, *and there were none from Madigan or even Kimble!* His clerk hurried in looking worried.

'Chief, Senator Harris Ferguson is outside, wanting to see you.' Lowering his voice he added, 'He's just been appointed the new head of Internal Security for the President . . . got his bodyguard along 'n' everything.'

'What's that in your hand?' Parminter was more interested in the paper Milton held than a politician.

The clerk held out a telegraph form. 'From Kimble. Just arrived.'

Parminter almost tore the yellow form as he opened it and read:

TRACED MAN NAMED VANCE TO TRINITY BASIN. BELIEVE
HIM TO BE BRONCO MADIGAN. MORE LATER.
KIMBLE

'What the hell does this mean?' Parminter growled.

'Chief!' the clerk ventured. 'The senator. . . ?'

Parminter sighed. 'All right. Bring him in.'

As if he didn't have enough on his plate. Missing marshals, a sudden spate of large-scale hold-ups and robberies all over the north-west, and now a damn Senator preening himself because he'd just received a top appointment by Congress! Gonna waste time he couldn't spare!

But he managed a welcoming smile as the clerk opened the door and Senator Ferguson swept in, his usual impeccable self, wearing a pearl-grey suit and Homburg, and carrying his signature silver-topped cane. He seated himself without greeting, looking very serious.

'Miles, this Johnny True thing: there's been a significant development I think you should know about.

And it's going to knock you on your rear-end.'

Inwardly, Parminter groaned. *What the hell else was going to jump up and demand his attention when all he wanted to do was locate his two best marshals?*

But he put on his best face. 'I'm all ears, Senator, and by the way, congratulations on your appointment. . . .'

Damn protocol!

CHAPTER 10

BOUNTY

'Madigan? Your name is not Vance?'

Merida Alvarez looked puzzledly at Vance, flicked her eyes to Kimble who was more or less staying in the background. They were all three seated in the small kitchen at the A-Star ranch.

When Kimble had released Vance from the cells, and after sending a wire to headquarters, the man had vetoed the idea of going back to the young marshal's hotel. 'I'd rather get back to Merida's spread, Beau. Kelso's mighty vindictive and Mitch Hanlon can't be depended on to give her any protection.'

Kimble had agreed, giving the man a twisted smile as he said, 'Another Madigan trait: protect the help-less!'

Vance had thrown him a steady, almost bitter look. 'It's the only way I know. Whatever name I'm stuck with.'

'Look, Bronco, I'm not trying to rile you, but you

are serious about completely losing your memory, aren't you?'

Vance laughed shortly. 'You seem to know more about me than I know myself – answer your own question.'

'Well, it was a stupid question, I guess.' Kimble sounded truly contrite. 'But it'd explain so much. Especially why you never reported in about Johnny True. Parminter's practically wetting himself, waiting to hear something.'

Vance spread his hands. 'He better keep a spare pair of trousers handy then, There's nothing I can tell him.'

'You do want to recollect, don't you?'

'Now that *is* a stupid question. Why don't you tell me something about myself as we ride along. . . ?'

Kimble was eager enough. He related some of the things he and Madigan had done together, the gunfights, brawls, the wild chases with murderous lead flying about their ears, even their disagreements; Madigan's maverick style, his contempt for regulations and laws that bound a man's hands and sometimes allowed a criminal to escape justice.

'But not if you could help it,' Kimble added, as they neared the A-Star. 'Not too long ago a man named Estrada seemed to be untouchable by American law and was on his way to South America, but you borrowed my Mannlicher rifle and my new German telescopic sight to "hunt antelope", you said. Estrada was shot from a great distance on a sailing ship. Greater than any regular Western rifle could reach.'

Vance hipped around to look into Kimble's face, his

frown deep. 'I guess that better be enough. My head's aching something fierce. . . .'

They rode the rest of the way in silence. Kimble had plenty to think about. So far he hadn't gotten much reaction out of 'Vance'. *There had to be some way to tap into that clouded mind, surely?*

But, watching Vance in the kitchen now as Merida set coffee before them, Kimble saw something he had never seen before, not in Bronco Madigan: the way those bullet eyes softened and warmed as they followed the Mexican girl's movements, the unconscious easing of the iron jaw, the general relaxing of the rawhide body. Very *un*-Madigan! This man, whoever he was, cared more than a little for the woman.

Kimble had never thought he would ever see the day when that happened. Madigan had always refused to allow himself to become involved emotionally: he did his job and moved on. Though Kimble suspected that now and again Madigan had slipped a few dollars here and there to people he figured deserved a little more help, or returned on the quiet to lend a hand, above and beyond the call of duty.

But this feeling for the girl was plain for anyone to see and Kimble was sure the Madigan he had known would have kept his guard up and never have let such feelings show.

What was more, he sensed that the girl knew and had no objections. He suddenly realized that Merida was speaking to him now. 'You say you are Vance's friend, but you know him as Bronco Madigan. Obviously, he has no memory of you or what you have

126

so far told him of his life as a federal marshal, is there some medical help that will bring back his memory?'

'I don't know, Merida. There are doctors in Europe who have a different approach to medicine in general than we do here. They work a lot with the mind.' He hesitated. 'My father brought one such man out from Vienna when I had . . . a problem. I'm not sure whether he actually *did* anything, apart from instilling in me the desire to cure myself. And I suppose that was what my father had paid for, anyway.' He could see she was puzzled and he said, quietly and quickly, 'I was heading into alcoholism. The doctor didn't give me any medication, but spoke with me for many hours; made me talk about myself and my problems. That kind of thing wouldn't work in Bronco's situation because he recalls nothing.'

The girl frowned, looking disappointed. 'Oh. I would gladly sell the ranch if the money could be used to find a doctor who would help. And also there is the money you insisted I take, Vance, that your friend Thunder gave you.'

My God! She must care mighty strongly for him! was Kimble's first thought, swinging his gaze quickly to Vance.

The man frowned. 'I couldn't and won't let you do that, Merida!'

'For Heaven's sake, why not!' the sounded almost angry. 'If it would solve your problems!'

'You dunno anything about me,' he said roughly. 'I killed Tully and Ferris in a fair fight, despite what Dade McLintock thinks. I tracked down three murdering snakes in Wyoming and I killed them, too, in a shoot-out. I don't feel anything about either of those things, except satisfaction. Those men deserved to die and I'm glad I was the one to kill them. Now what kind of a man does that make me?'

Vance looked from the girl to Kimble, who replied, 'A damn good marshal, Bronco. In fact, you were – sorry, *are* – Chief Parminter's top man. You see? Your memory might be blacked-out right now, but your instincts are the same, your general character doesn't seem to have changed very much.'

' "Much", Beau? That means you figure there are some changes.'

Kimble waved it aside airily. 'You know what I mean. You're basically the same man – just that you have a temporary block. And maybe a slightly different slant on life in general.'

The others saw the haunted look briefly in his eyes before he made an effort to hide it. 'I'm not sure that I want to be this Madigan from what I've heard so far.'

Kimble tensed, not believing his ears.

But Merida closed her small hand over Vance's fingers on the table. 'I know you as Vance and I like what I know. You have been good to me – and to your friend, Thunder. I don't need to know about your past.'

'But I do,' Kimble said curtly. 'And so does Bronco. He's made a lot of enemies over the years, Merida, if he doesn't recognize one sometime, it could cost him his life.'

The concern washed quickly over the girl's face and the golden skin took on a slight pallor. '*Madre de Dios!*'

Vance patted her hand briefly, speaking to Kimble.

'There's just nothing I can help you with, Beau – I don't even recognize you. You're as much a stranger to me now as when you walked into that cell block. Nothing you've said has meant a thing to me.'

'That's what I mean when I say we have to talk about your past, Bronco! I know plenty about you, from the last two years that I've worked with you and from reports of your earlier years in the Marshals' Service. There must be something there, some *key*, that will trigger your memory.'

'It – it sounds logical, Vance,' Merida said quietly.

'Yeah, I guess so – but maybe later.'

'Later? Listen, man, this Johnny True is out to wreak some kind of massive havoc! We've got to know what you've found out so we can stop him!'

Kimble didn't like the stony look on Vance's face.

'Beau, it's not part of my world right now. Too bad, maybe, but it's a fact.' Vance drove a stiffened finger hard against the deal table top. 'This is where my life is – I've hired on to help Merida. Her troubles with Kelso, and anyone else, come first.'

Beau Kimble writhed on the chair, mouth tight, wanting to cuss but making an effort not to in front of the uncomfortable-looking girl.

'Bronco – Vance! Whatever you want to call yourself! It can't be that way! *You are a United States marshal!* You took an oath of office. You've stuck by it for twenty years! You – you can't just ignore it and say it doesn't matter anymore, that Merida's problems are more important! They aren't!'

'They damn well are to her!'

'OK, I give you that. But, it's the bigger picture,

Bronco. Look, this Johnny True is a notorious killer who's been operating here and in Mexico, South America, even Europe, for years and he's never been caught. Now, we know he's been or is being, paid a *half-of-a-million* dollars for whatever job he's been hired to do! For that kind of money it – well, it beggars the mind to even think what he might be capable of!' The young marshal swept an arm around the crudely built room. 'And you think whatever trouble there is here, in this out-of-the-way basin, deserves your attention more than the other. . . ?'

Vance shrugged. 'For me, Beau, there is no "other" – I know nothing about it. I can't help you. Why should I waste my time puzzling over it when I can be helping Merida?'

Merida looked decidedly uneasy now and Kimble sighed heavily, threw up his arms. 'Well, I'm going to have to stick around no matter what. So you'd better tell me the situation here and I'll do what I can to help, too.'

Merida smiled and kissed him lightly on the cheek. 'You, too, are a good man, I think, Beaumont Kimble.'

He glared at Vance. 'I had a good teacher! And he doesn't even remember his star pupil!'

Nathan Kelso stepped out of the telegraph office, tugging on his soft leather riding gloves. He was wearing embossed half-leg riding boots, striped trousers with a grey waistcoat buttoned over a cream-coloured shirt. There was a pale-green neckerchief at his throat.

He was a man who liked to remind folk constantly that he was the richest and most powerful man in

Trinity Basin. He adjusted his grey curl-brim hat with the banded edge and looked about him. Sheriff McLintock, sitting a buckskin mount, walked it across to where the rancher waited, leading a saddled palomino, Kelso's own special horse.

The rancher mounted easily despite his bulk and settled into the hand-made saddle, specially built to accommodate his large backside. As they walked their horses away from the telegraph office which was just outside the town, close to the stage depot, the sheriff asked, 'Who'd you wire?'

Kelso glared coldly but said, 'You have no sense of discretion or even manners, Dade!'

McLintock shrugged his big shoulders. 'I've been told before. Who'd you send the wire to? Friends of that feller who used to wear pink shirts?'

Kelso chuckled. 'You are not as dumb as you make yourself appear, Dade, and I think I like that. Colorado Dukes led a wild bunch, now taken over by his son, Mason, I guess. He's already put a bounty on Madigan for killing his father.'

'He was pretty popular, huh? This Colodrado Dukes?'

'He was feared. Some say the boy's not quite right.' Kelso tapped his temple. 'Something of a maddog.'

McLintock grunted. 'Well, I din' know Dukes but I've seen dodgers on him from time to time. How come you knew a snake like that?'

Kelso smiled crookedly, shaking his head. 'You see what I mean about "no discretion", Dade? Well, probably you don't, so we'll let it slide. Let's just say that quite a long time ago I was in a . . . business arrange-

ment with the Dukes family up north. We had a difference of opinion and I – er – thought it best that I
move south. As it happened, I prospered while the
Dukes ran more and more afoul of the law, had their
numbers reduced to just Colorado and young Mace at
one time. You've likely heard of their gang's exploits.'

'Yeah: another bank robbed, stage held-up, even a
pay train derailed just a while back – and dead men
everywhere.'

Kelso frowned slightly. 'I still have a few contacts up
that way. From what I've heard over the past few
months, the Dukes gang have been on a veritable orgy
of robberies. The reward for their capture is now very
substantial.'

McLintock's glance was sharp. 'Now that sounds
interestin'.'

Kelso shook his head. 'I wouldn't think you'd be
able to claim a federal reward, but young Mace Dukes
has a bounty of his own out: for the man who finds
Madigan.'

Slowly, McLintock smiled. 'You sly ol' sidewinder,
Nate! You're gonna claim it, ain't you!'

Kelso didn't deny it. 'It never hurts to stay on the
right side of someone as unstable as Mason Dukes –
and if I can profit by it, get rid of the marshal in a way
that can never be traced to me, well, why not?'

'Like I said, a sly of sidewinder!'

'You could've chosen your words better, Dade! But
I'm in a mood good enough to let it pass. I think
within a week or two I ought to be in full control, if
not ownership, of A-Star, and that Mexican bitch will
be finished here once and for all! And Trinity Basin

will revert to being as it should be: entirely Anglo!'

Kimble speaking:

'I rolled deeper into the cave where the roof sloped down, clutching my Mannlicher rifle tightly. Bullets fired from outside screamed and caromed off the low, jagged roof and I yelled, "Bronco, I'm hit!"

' "Get the hell outa there! Worst place you can be in." Madigan's gun triggered and one of the killers outside yelled as he fell out of a tree. The Senator, shaking, scared white, brought up his shotgun. Bissom, outside, fired two shots and cut him down. He fell with a choking sound.

'Madigan dragged his rifle around one-handed, but he was too close to the rock wall and it jarred from his grip. Bissom and Kiley charged recklessly up the slope and came bursting into the cave blazing guns in their hands. Madigan dived towards them from the side, six-gun thrust out ahead of him, triggering. Bissom lurched, crouched, but Kiley staggered as Madigan dropped and fired his last bullet into the man. As Kiley went down, Bissom rose from his crouch, throwing down on Madigan. It hurt my bleeding side but I lifted my Mannlicher and triggered. Bissom's head exploded like a dropped melon.

'Madigan got to his feet amongst the choking gunsmoke and bodies, waved a hand to clear a patch, and saw I was down on my side, blood on the ground beneath me. . . .'

Kimble paused, then said, 'That was some shoot-out, Bronco! My first real one with you on assignment.'

In Merida's small bunkhouse, Kimble smiled wryly at the expression on Vance's face. The man had listened closely to the young marshal relating a violent incident that had taken place at the end of their first assignment together, but Kimble wasn't sure that it meant anything to him. The telling of such incidents over the past few days actually seemed to irritate Vance.

'You doctored me pretty roughly, and when I complained you told me to shut up, and not gripe at "every little gunshot wound".' Beau laughed shortly. 'I had nine buckshot pellets in me and two bullet holes! That was your idea of a "little" gunshot wound.'

'Sounds a mite rough,' Vance admitted, not all that interested. It wiped the smile from Kimble's face.

'You don't remember we both were almost fired because the Senator was killed while we were supposed to be protecting him?'

Vance rubbed his forehead, shook his head slowly. 'Beau, I don't recall that cave, or any of the other places you've told me about the last few days.'

Kimble's shoulders slumped. 'Well, there are other times. Maybe if I went into greater detail. . . ?'

'Forget it, Beau!' Vance snapped. 'Face up to it: I'm not this Madigan you keep trying to convince me I am.'

'You *are!* And I damn well aim to prove it!'

'Beau, I might've *been* Madigan once. I don't recall. But whoever he was, he's gone now – I'm not him any longer. I'm Vance whoever *he* is! I have no past and God alone knows whether I have a future. But I'd be almighty obliged if you'd just *shut up* and get off the damned subject! I'm sick of hearing about Madigan! I don't know him and I don't want to. Just leave me be.'

CHAPTER 11

MAD DOG

Mace Dukes, stark naked and holding a cocked six-gun wrenched open the door of the room. He thrust the Colt through the opening and the man who stood there leapt back, white as the pale body of the saloon girl lounging on the crumpled sheets and scattered pillows in the background.

'It better be *damn* good!' Mace snapped in his girl-ish voice, the acne pits standing out against his flushed, pinched face. 'Why you interrupt me, feller?'

The man in the passage, held out his right hand and it shook like a bush in the cold wind that howled outside the grimy windows. 'W-wire for you, Mr Dukes . . . marked "Urgent".'

Mace Dukes snatched the folded yellow paper and used his tongue and teeth to open it out while the messenger stood there trembling under the cocked Colt. Dukes squinted at the words, lips moving as he read laboriously. When he looked up he was smiling –

if the slight parting of the razor-like slash could be called that. He pursed those same lips and suddenly fisted-up the front of the startled messenger's shirt and yanked him into the room, kicking the door closed. The man's eyes bulged as he saw the naked girl now sitting up quickly on the rumpled bed.

'I ain't got any change right now,' Mace said, sneering. He gestured to the whore with his gun. 'You can have ten minutes with her by way of a tip.'

'Now, just a minute. . . !' she began to protest, but Dukes's attention was taken by the messenger who was fumbling at the door handle. 'Where the hell you goin'?'

'I-I'm a married man, Mr Dukes! I-I don't have no truck with . . . whores!'

'That so?' The gun barrel came up and jammed under the man's jaw, Mace pressing him against the wall. 'Well, no one balks at any offer I make, friend – start takin' off your pants!'

'No, please, Mr—!'

'Just a minute, you little runt!' snapped the girl, standing now and reaching for her soiled robe. 'If you think I'm lettin' him near me just because you say so—'

The walls reverberated to the explosion of the six-gun and the messenger fell to his knees in fright. A red spot appeared just above the cleft of the woman's breasts and her eyes bulged as her painted mouth gaped and she was driven back across the bed. She rolled off the far side and thudded to the floor. 'Don't call me runt, you slut!'

The terrified messenger started to plead with Dukes as the man turned to him. 'You're outa luck, fella.

Mebbe next time. But so's you remember your manners and don't turn down what I offer—'

The gun barrel whipped back and forth on the kneeling man's head, knocking his hat halfway across the room. His face was a torn bloody mess when the door burst open and two of Dukes's men, obviously hurriedly dressed, came in with drawn guns.

'You OK, Mace?' a big man asked, square-jawed and beetle-browed. They called him 'Monte The Mountain'.

Mace Dukes casually kicked the moaning man on the floor and waved the crumpled telegraph form. 'I'm OK now, Monte! An old friend – well, a kinda friend – has just sent me word that that bastard Madigan's still alive!'

'Alive?' the big man repeated, obviously surprised.

Mace nodded, face tight and ugly now, unworried by the crowd that was gathering outside the room. 'Not for long! Go round up the boys – like the geese, we're goin' south for the winter.'

Rico Alvarez was anxiously standing in Kelso's ranch office. He had been offered the best leather chair in the room but he had too much nervous energy raging through his lean young body to stay still.

Kelso glanced up from his desk. He swiftly hid the angry look in his eyes, forced a smile and a mild tone. 'I'm sorry I can't offer you any wine, Rico, but you once told me you only drink a special kind.'

'*Si* – a vintage laid down by my ancestors which they brought originally from Spain, to California, then to here.' He cut a decent enough figure with his medium-tall leanness in the Spanish riding clothes. There was a quirt on his left wrist and he slapped this nervously and irritatingly against the top of his high riding boot.

Kelso's face straightened. 'Yeah. I sometimes forget you've got real Spanish blood running in your veins.' Kelso stood up, offering the paper he held. 'Read this and see if it satisfies you.' As Rico took it looking puzzled, he added, 'It's a bill of sale for A-Star. You're selling to me for a price we can negotiate – and I reckon you won't be disappointed with your share.'

'But this cannot be! *I* can sign, yes, but my sister must sign, too.'

Kelso moved closer, smiling again, slipping an arm about the young man's narrow shoulders. 'Rico, some time back you agreed to help me buy A-Star. Well, time's passing and I can't wait forever. You've had no success talking your sister around to selling.'

'She is influenced by those *gringos!*' Rico said sharply. 'She regards this Vance more than favourably, and the other, Kimble, he, too, advises Merida not to sell. I am only a boy in their eyes and am ignored. . . .'

'Sure, I understand that, Rico. You're young and you want the easy life your ancestors planned for you. Your sister was very lucky she was able to wheedle that small section of land out of the territorial government, you know, but now I want it back – and you promised to help. You said you never break your word.'

Rico seemed uneasy. '*Si.* I-I thought if you pay enough Merida and I can go to relatives in California where we will be welcomed into the old style of living. . . .'

'Yeah, yeah, that'd be fine. But first your sister has to sell.' Kelso tapped ther paper. 'Now you sign and we have a deal.'

Rico was perplexed. 'But if only I sign. . . .'

'Rico, *amigo*, you must know your sister's signature well by now! After all the papers both of you had to sign when she was fighting to get back A-Star land.'

The youth was horrified. 'You wish me to *forge Merida's name?*'

'Well, I guess it's up to you, I'm just putting a suggestion to you. But it'll settle things once and for all and I can pay you cash money, Rico. You and Merida could be on your way to California within a week, maybe only a few days . . . You know it's the kind of life she deserves, rather than trying to build a ranch from scratch, working like a peasant all those long hours.'

'These men – this Vance and Kimble – they have fired Mitch Hanson who was too lazy and they are building the ranch into shape, capturing wild *caballos*. Vance is a fine horse breaker and soon there will be a fine big herd to sell. . . .'

'Rico, this is my final offer. Today's the day. No more after this. And if I have to go to the law to help me, and Dade McLintock and a certain judge *are* on my side, you and Merida could come out with practically nothing. I'm trying to give you a break, kid.'

Rico was sick with worry. 'But Vance and his friend . . . they are lawmen!'

Kelso smiled. 'Don't worry about them. They won't interfere.'

'But they are hard *hombres!* They practise with their

guns and shoot *magnifico. . . .*'

'I said to forget 'em.' Kelso tapped the Cattlemen's Association calendar on the wall beside him. 'See that big X there? That's marking today's date. I'm expecting some friends to help me – er – finalize things with A-Star. They're a new crew and should arrive at any time. I'm telling you, Rico, there's nothing to worry about. Oh, you might not like what I'm asking you to do, but you'll have what you want and you know things will be better for your sister if you take her to your kinfolk. That's the kind of thing a young *caballero* could be proud of. It would earn you respect!'

Rico paced restlessly and, when his back was turned, Kelso's face was ugly: he looked like he wanted to kick the youth. But when Rico turned, he put on a bland, friendly look.

'Time's running out, boy,' Kelso said, hardening his tone a little, deciding Rico had had enough soft-soaping.

Rico swallowed, hands shaking as he lifted the bill of sale and started to re-read it. Kelso strode back behind his desk, dipped the pen in the inkwell and held it out, face grim.

'This is it, Rico! I see the dust of my friends' horses out there. Here! Now, sign! Or get out with your pockets empty!'

Vance and Kimble were working on a second corral at A-Star. Merida was somewhere in the house, cooking or tidying, or doing whatever she had to do. She made sure they had regular meals and good ones, too: mostly Mexican-style which appealed to Kimble – and he remembered that Madigan, too liked the Spanish spices and ingredients. Yet, while Vance ate readily enough it seemed to be mostly because he was hungry from the long hours of ranch work, rather than with any real relish. He used food merely to replace energy used.

Once again, he had that faint uneasy stirring within: could he be mistaken? *No*, he told himself. This man was Bronco Madigan. He *looked* like him despite his gauntness. His memory had gone temporarily, that was all: he hoped! It was bound to change some things about him, even though earlier he had assured Vance that, essentially, his character was pretty much the same. And there was the girl and 'Vance's' interest in her.

'Ah, to hell with it,' Kimble said aloud and picked up the saw to cut off the end of the lodgepole he had been measuring. A sawtooth pricked his thumb. 'Goddamnit to hell!'

Vance looked up and rested on the crowbar at the posthole he was digging. 'I get the notion that cussing doesn't come naturally to you, Beau.'

Kimble looked up, surprised, smiled thinly. 'Was never given much to cursing – till I joined up as your partner.'

Vance grunted, started digging again. 'Seems right handy that you can throw the blame for your short-comings onto a man who's got no comeback.'

'I didn't mean it that way – I'm not carping. Just trying to keep reminding you of things I know about you.'

'You *think* you know about me.'

142

Kimble gave him a crooked smile. 'Oh, I know 'em all right, Bronco. You'll remember in time.'

Vance grunted, kept digging. 'What'd you say in that wire you sent before we left town?'

Kimble had been waiting for him to ask. *That* was like Madigan, holding back his curiosity. 'Just that I thought I'd located our missing marshal – Bronco Madigan. I said I'd send more information, but I don't really have any.' He tossed aside the off-cut from the pole, took a rasp and smoothed away the splinters from the sawcut. 'I wish I did, Bronco.'

Vance stopped digging, catching the other's gaze. 'You trying to tell me you finally believe I ain't ever going to remember?'

'I'm no doctor! What do I know? But I think you should come back to Washington with me and—'

'Leave it, Beau,' Vance cut in coldly. 'I told you to quit on that and I've given you some leeway, but here's where it ends.'

Kimble stiffened. Vance meant it. He knew the man's headaches were easing some but he often saw Vance staring into space, rubbing hard at temples and forehead, watched him sway as if with dizziness. God knew what went on in that churned-up mind. He made queer mumblings in his sleep, too. Maybe it was all working towards the memory regenerating.

'That's Rico's Ay-rab!'

Kimble snapped his head up, stared in the direction Vance was looking. There was a rider coming in over the ridge between here and the creek boundary with Flying K.

The man was doubled over, swaying dangerously in

the saddle. Vance dropped the crowbar and began to run towards the high-stepping Arab.

'It's Rico – looks like he's hurt!'

Rico didn't like the look of Kelso's 'friends' when they came into the ranch office. Rough, sweaty, dirty men, but what scared him most, they were all gun-hung. The young one with the acned face and the scary eyes glanced around the room, dwarfed by the towering man with the square jaw standing behind him.

Kelso looked a little wary, too, and nodded, forcing a stiff smile. 'You'd be young Mason. You were barely out of short pants when I last saw you.'

Mace's thin, ugly face snapped around towards the rancher. 'Lucky for you. If I'd been just a bit bigger I'd've likely kicked your butt – I've hated smart-mouths all my life.'

The men crowded in: Rico wasn't sure how many but he thought seven or eight. Suddenly he pulled the bill of sale towards him, picked up the pen and signed swiftly. He left the paper on the desk and spoke to Kelso.

'I have signed the paper, *señor*, I must leave now.'

Mace Dukes stepped into his path.'What's your hurry, pretty-boy? Bad manners to run out on guests.'

Kelso cleared his throat. 'He's a neighbour – just had some paperwork to do. No need for him to stick around.'

'Yeah?' Mace picked up the bill of sale and without taking his eyes off Kelso, passed it over his shoulder to the big man. 'Monte, take a look at this.'

They were all crowding around now, hemming in

Kelso, sensing some fun here. 'Looks like someone's buyin' a ranch.'

'Yeah?' Mason Dukes flicked his awful eyes to Kelso. 'You got money to do that?'

'Well, I was planning on using part of the reward for finding Madigan for you.' Kelso was getting his confidence back, but this motley crew had him on edge: most of his men were working on the range, rounding-up steers. He felt vulnerable. And Mace Dukes sure looked loco. . . .

Big Monte suddenly glanced up, shook the paper. 'Some gal's gotta sign this yet.'

Kelso's face straightened and he snatched the paper from Monte's huge hand. 'Damn! Rico, you stupid son of a bitch! You've got to sign for Merida – where the hell is he?'

'The kid?' asked one man with a wall-eye. 'He went out the side door. Looked like he was gonna be sick. . . .'

'Judas! Stop him!' Kelso snapped.'I'm not finished with him yet. . . .'

'Reckon you are.' Mace was leaning out the window, seeing Rico swinging aboard his Arab mount and raking with the big silver spurs. Mace's six-gun came blurring up and he snapped two fast shots.

Rico jerked and swayed, almost fell from the saddle, but he lay along the horse's straining neck, lashing with his quirt. The animal made it fast beyond the corrals and swung around the back of the barn as two more men started shooting.

'Goddamnit! Quit that!' snapped Mace, once again cursing his thin voice. 'That's a good-lookin' hoss.

Reckon I'll pick it up later. Meanwhile . . .' He turned and rammed the smoking Colt into the startled Kelso's midriff. 'You claimin' the reward I put up for findin' Pa's killer, huh?'

'That – that's the deal I had in mind.' Kelso was sweating again, shaken because he had lost control here.

'Uh-huh. Well, I don't like you, Kelso. Never did. Pa an' Uncle Pete never had a good word to say about you, neither. Said you run off with some of their *dinero* . . . about the time a posse found the hideout and Uncle Pete and a lot more of our kin was killed. Pa always said you musta set the posse onto us.'

'No! No, I swear, Mace! I admit I took the cashbox but there wasn't more'n a few hundred. I invested in the beef market – that's how I made my money. But I swear I never sold you out!'

'But you're still tryin' to make money outa Pa!'

'Just trying to help you, Mace—'

'Hogwash! Helpin' yourself!' Mace bored those murderous eyes into Kelso's for a long minute, then every man in the room jumped as Dukes's Colt exploded, the roar muffled by Kelso's thick body, muzzle pressed against his heavy belly.

Men scattered and some stumbled as Kelso was blown backwards, fell to his knees, grasping his bleeding stomach, sobbing in pain.

'Now that wound'll kill you, Nate, ol' pal, but it'll take time. An' durin that time, I'm gonna ask you some questions – startin' with where I'll find this snake Madigan. . . ? 'Course, I might have to jog your memory a little bit – huh?'

Kelso screamed as Mace dug his hands into the bloody wound. The others gathered round quickly: they *knew* good ol' Mace would find something to keep them amused.

CHAPTER 12

TRUE LIES

Rico Alvarez had bled a lot from the wound in his side. Merida fussed over him as he lay stretched out on his bed in his room at the ranch.

Vance and Kimble stood at the window, both with rifles, trying to hear what Rico was saying to his sister.

'Kelso tried to get me to forge your signature on a bill of sale for the ranch – but I signed only my own name and ran away while Kelso and his visitors were talking.'

'Who were his visitors?' Kimble asked quickly.

Rico replied, but was gasping a little as Merida tied off the bandage over his wound. 'They – frightened me! Dirty, terrible men, all with guns. . . .'

'Who were they, kid?' Vance asked quietly, trying to break through the boy's terror and shock from the bullet wound: his first.

'The leader – Mason?' He touched his face. 'Much *acne.*'

'Mason Dukes!' breathed Kimble. 'My God, Bronco!

Last we heard of you, officially, you were following a lead to Colorado Dukes – who'd worked with Johnny True before – and a man who favoured pink shirts!'

Vance frowned. 'What're you getting at?'

'Suppose after you killed Colorado in a gunfight, you dressed in his shirt so when approaching the gang's hideout in Red Canyon they'd think it was him returning? But they recognized you and shot you.' He touched his head.

Vance's face was blank. Seeing Kimble's disappointment, Merida said, her hand on Vance's arm. 'If you were – are – a marshal, it *sounds* possible, Vance.'

'Merida, it means nothing to me. But right now we've got more to worry about than my memory.'

He drew the curtain aside, revealing a roiling cloud of dust as riders came thundering down the same slope Rico had used earlier.

'*Madre de Dios!*' breathed Merida. 'I count eight!'

'If that's Mace Dukes's bunch we're in a lot of trouble!' Kimble gritted.

Vance half-dragged the girl across the room and through the door into the parlour. 'Bring every gun you have and all the bullets you can lay your hands on.'

She hurried to obey as he strode to the front, dropped the bar in place on the door. There was no point in closing the windows. In the kitchen, he barred the door there and pushed the heavy table against it.

None of these precautions would be very effective but they had to be taken.He paused to glance out the living-room window and saw the men dismounting in the yard, scattering for cover behind the barn and the corral rails. He counted five: the other three must already be around the back.

Then the first shot shattered a window beside the front door and a girlish voice called, 'Don' wanna hurt the gal or that kid. Just wanna see Madigan step out onto the porch. Oh, and that other sonofabitchin' marshal you got hidin' in there!'

Vance crouched and duck-walked towards the broken window. Kimble's voice answered. 'You're tangling with Federal Law here, Mace! Better think about that!'

Dukes laughed and a few of the men with him joined in. 'That you, Madigan?'

'Kimble here – US Marshal. Heed what I say, Mace!'

'You heed what *I* say!' and what he said must have made Merida's ears burn. Vance rose from his crouch and triggered four fast shots, raking the barn where he judged Dukes and his men were holed-up. Splinters flew and someone shouted a startled epithet.

'*That* was Madigan!' Kimble called. 'You won't find us a pushover, Mace!'

Mace Dukes cursed fluently again. 'Changed my mind – the gal's in it, too! This is her place. Madigan's been workin' here, undercover, so she's gonna get what's comin' to her, too! I'll be generous, though: you got two minutes to step out onto the porch, Madigan! More chance than you gave my pa!'

'Don't remember him,' Vance called. 'But he must've been scum to sire you.'

A savage volley raked the house.

Vance bellied across the room to where a wide-eyed

Merida crouched in the arched doorway. She had several cartons of bullets at her feet, and two hand-guns beside them, one a Colt, the other a Remington. She held a Winchester carbine and had rested a single-shot .20 gauge shotgun against the door frame, just outside the kitchen. *It might be enough.*

'Go to the root cellar, Merida,' Vance told her, as Kimble began shooting and the men outside poured another volley into the house, urged on by a scream-ing Mace Dukes.

'This is my home, Vance! I will fight for it!'

'It's too dangerous up here!'

Suddenly she stood, the carbine flashing to her shoulder and she fired two fast shots. A window shat-tered behind Vance. As he whirled a man cried out and he glimpsed a shadow falling across the cracked glass. He snapped his head back to a quizzical Merida and said, 'OK! You made your point! But find some decent cover: that heavy dresser there.'

Bullets raked the wall and splinters flew, china orna-ments shattered, lead ricocheted. Pots and pans clat-tered and bounced. Vance ran to the front of the house, hearing Kimble shooting to the rear. A man, crouched double, was running into the barn. Vance snapped a hurried shot, the man took a tumble, but he managed to crawl behind a wooden feed bin. Vance's next shot tore a long splinter from the edge but the wounded man did not fire back.

Kimble's rifle hammered and one of the three men at the rear staggered out from behind the old cask he had been using as shelter. He held a shotgun and trig-gered even as he began to fall. Buckshot smashed in an entire windowframe, showering Kimble with glass, splinters and smouldering curtains. He thrashed to get free and in doing so exposed himself in the bullet-pocked frame.

Two guns thundered out in the yard and a sliver of wood flew up from the window ledge and ripped across his lower face. He lurched, grasping at the jagged splinter protruding from his jaw. Two more shots cracked and he jerked as lead burned across the tip of his shoulder. His head wrenched aside and a second slug missed him by the thickness of a cigarette paper. He fell to hands and knees, hung there, trying to breathe, grimacing as he worked at the splinter, his blood pouring down his neck and soaking his shirt collar.

Merida ran to another window. A man was dropping the sliprails of the corral, chasing out the remuda, jumping and slapping his hat wildly. He turned the horses keeping them between himself and the house. She knew he would be clinging to the red mare's flying mane, legs lifted off the ground, letting the running mount carry him closer to the house.

Vance had seen the same manoeuvre and unhesitatingly shot the mare through the head. The man screamed as the animal fell on him, pinning him. He thrashed and groaned briefly, then was still. Vance swung his smoking rifle onto the barn where he could hear Dukes yelling orders and abuse. The man's voice was too high-pitched and excited to make out what he was saying.

But Vance knew then that the stampeding horses had been a diversion. Two men used long-handled rakes to push the barn doors open and then a buck-board stacked with hessian bags and bales of hay rolled foward. It gathered speed as the men behind it strained and shoved it into the yard, setting it rumbling towards the front of the house.

Vance crouched, trying to see their legs, fired and saw dust spurt from a wheel spoke, inches off. The buckboard didn't falter. Then he saw the smoke. It rose from amongst the bales of hay. An instant later flames erupted and engulfed the fodder, a roaring fully-born blaze.

'Root cellar! *Now!*' Vance yelled at the startled girl. She was frozen, watching as the now flaming vehicle rumbled and crashed into the front porch. The burn-ing hay bales jumped loose, piled onto and around the porch steps. The vehicle spun and tilted onto its side. The men scattered and Vance called for Kimble to start shooting. He got off a couple of hurried shots himself, sent two men spinning, then grabbed the girl and dragged her into the kitchen. He hauled up the trapdoor to the root cellar and practically threw her down the steps, starting to drop the door back into place.

Then the yard door suddenly crashed open and Monte the Mountain filled the now-splintered frame, bracing a shotgun into his hip. With a throaty roar he flung the heavy kitchen table aside effortlessly. Vance dropped as the shotgun thundered, hurled hot and whistling buckshot into the room. Lead balls screeched as they struck the big stove, clattered amongst the pots, making them leap and spin. Vance triggered his rifle upwards, got off a single shot and then the hammer fell on an empty breech. He hurled the weapon away, rolling swiftly across the floor, fumbled for his Colt but it had fallen from the holster. Monte staggered as the rifle bullet hit him, but he bared his teeth in a cold murderous grin as he tracked Vance's rolling body with the second barrel of the Greener.

Then from the half-raised trapdoor Merida's carbine crashed again and again, driving almost a full magazine into The Mountain. Monte was tough and could take a lot of punishment, but with a couple of pounds of lead smashing into him he shook like a giant doll. Roaring and wrenching his huge body, he lifted his weapon. Vance snatched the shotgun still leaning against the arched doorway as Monte lined-up on the frozen girl. Vance triggered and Monte was blown back violently into the yard.

Vance yelled at Merida to get back into the cellar, found his six-gun and dived through the doorway, rolling. He glimpsed a pimply-faced youth standing there, legs braced, a Colt in each fist, buck teeth showing in a ragged smile as he swung the guns to bear. 'Madigan! Die you bastard!'

Still skidding through the dust, Vance fired and his lead jerked the killer off the ground, throwing his aim. Vance shot him again and he twisted with a mighty effort and got off a shot from his left-hand gun – then was smashed to the ground by a rifle bullet from the house. He somersaulted and landed face down, unmoving, like a bundle of dirty rags.

Vance saw Kimble at a window, with a smoking rifle, a jagged wound across his face spurting blood all over him. He started to run, but Merida was already easing Kimble down with his back against the wall. The young marshal lifted a hand weakly: signalling that he was OK.

Vance ran around to the porch where the fire was roaring up the support posts, burning the door, but so far had failed to ignite the grass growing on the sod roof. Rico was at the horse trough, barely able to stand, trying to fill a wooden pail, using his good arm, steadying the pail with the wounded one. Vance saw a wounded outlaw at the barn door lifting a six-gun and killed him with two hammering shots. He quickly checked the back, saw two more dead men, then eased Rico aside and took the bucket as the boy fainted.

'You did all right, Rico. Lucky the porch is mostly adobe.' He sloshed the first of many buckets onto the flames.

It was almost sundown and the remuda was still loose. But the horses wouldn't go far and could easily be rounded-up come morning. The blackened porch and burnt-out wagon on its side, plus the dead bodies piled just inside the barn, were not exactly welcoming to any visitor.

Rico and Kimble's wounds had been taken care of. The young marshal was barely able to speak intelligibly, but his face would heal.

'The scar will make you more attractive to the ladies, I think, Beau,' Merida said with a smile, and Kimble grinned as well as he could.

Vance said, 'Beau don't need any advantages – all the gals want to mother him soon as they see that baby face.'

Beau looked at him quickly, his voice husky. 'You

remembering?' Vance curled a lip, reached for his reloaded Winchester where it leaned against the wall. 'Mace recognized you out there, Bronco.'

'He was so crazy with hate he'd've seen anyone as Madigan, just so long as he could shoot him.' Vance crouched by the window. The others heard it then: the sound of a rider coming into the yard.

It was Sheriff Dade McLintock and he came in through the sundown fire, throwing his weight around, immediately demanding to know what was going on.

Vance told him curtly. 'You'll find what's left of the Mason Dukes' gang piled up in the barn. What brings you out here, anyway?'

McLintock seemed more subdued. 'Been trouble over at Flyin' K. Kelso's dead. His men said Mason Dukes done it.' He took a telegraph form from his shirt pocket, waving it in Kimble's direction. 'I brung this for him.'

'But you took it to Kelso first,' Vance said, face hard. 'Found him dead, then figured you better get on the right side of the law by bringing Kimble's wire here.'

Dade flushed and Vance knew he was right, but the sheriff recovered, smoothed out the form and showed it around. 'Don't reckon Kelso'd've got much out of it.' The paper was covered in numbers. 'Operator brung it to me. He'd never seen nothin' like it – I figured it must be some kinda code.'

Kimble hesitated, then, reaching for the form, rasped, 'You recognize the Marshal's cipher, Bronco?' Vance looked blank and Kimble sighed. 'OK – I can work it out. Rico, I'll need your room.' Hobbling, the young Mexican led him to his room and Merida went to make coffee.

'Dukes lookin' for you, Vance?' the sheriff asked.

Vance shook his head. 'No. Someone named Madigan.'

Dade frowned. 'Thought that was you.'

'Why don't you go check the dead men, Dade? You'll need proper identification for your report. Could even be a reward you can claim part of. . . .'

McLintock hesitated, didn't care for the hard look on Vance's face but went out, mumbling, as Merida returned with a cloth to cover the bullet-chipped table. 'Are you going to see a doctor, now, Vance?'

Vance shrugged. 'What for? Wound's healing. I'm happy as I am—'

'Beau thinks you have started remembering.'

'He's guessing. He's bent my ear till it's numb about Madigan. I dunno what kinda life I had before, but the one this Madigan led sure don't appeal to me.'

'But . . . your whole life! You can't just continue without knowing what went before, Vance! It-it doesn't make sense! It will be so lonely for you. No memories!'

Vance smiled crookedly. 'I'm working on making some, Merida. Maybe memories we could share some-day.' There was something in his voice that made her heart pound. 'That's if you still need me around the ranch, *querida?*'

She smiled suddenly at the endearment. 'I will need a partner rather than a ranch hand – *querido mio.*'

He smiled crookedly. 'I was hoping so. Madigan could never hope for anything like this. His life wasn't the kind he could expect any woman to share. But even a man like him would grab with both hands if he ever saw such a once-in-a-liftime chance coming his ways. He'd be a damn fool to pass it up.'

Merida's lower lip was trembling. There was a warm glitter in her dark eyes as she reached out a hand tentatively and Vance took it slowly, held it, tightening his grip as if he would never let go.

They did not notice Kimble standing in the doorway. He stood watching a moment longer, looking very thoughtful as he entered and held out a sheet of paper with hand-printed words on it. In his husky voice he said, 'I've decoded Parminter's message. The Johnny True assignment has ended. He was hired by dissidents in Congress to assassinate the President. His fee, half-a million dollars, a quarter-million to be paid before the job, the rest immediately after it was done. The group had trouble raising the down-payment but True got his quarter-million. To raise the rest they hired the Dukes' gang to get it by a series of robberies, but Dukes kept the cash and the congressmen didn't dare touch them. Then Madigan upset things even more by tracking down Colorado Dukes, killed him in a gunfight, but was shot himself before he could tackle the rest of the gang.' Kimble paused and asked Merida to bring him a glass of water which he gulped down, smiling his thanks.

'It was a bad move altogether for the congressmen: Johnny True did not live up to his name. He must've known he could never really hope to get away with such an assassination, would never be able to work again, never know peace anywhere. And never have another chance to demand such a high fee. So, while they were running around trying to raise the second half of his money, he took his quarter-million and simply disappeared, leaving behind a list of the men who hired him.' Kimble smiled. 'I'll just bet Parminter loved that!' He spread his hands. 'So, True could be anywhere in the world by now. With that much money he can hide forever, never be heard from again. Parminter's happy to settle for that, and the names of the men who tried to hire him. So – case closed.'

'I'll bet Madigan would be glad to hear it, too,' Vance said quietly, holding Beau's gaze. 'He could relax with a clear conscience then, wherever he is.'

'Wouldn't be his style,' Kimble rasped, massaging his lower face, working his stiffening jaw, watching Vance closely.

'It'd be mine, if I was Madigan. After the kind of tough life he's led for twenty years, age slowing him down, all those old wounds giving him trouble. It'd be mighty hard to pass up the chance of some peace and a little happiness if it came his way at a point where he had a clean slate with the Marshals: all assignments completed. Wouldn't be surprised if he'd had a yearning for such things for a long time but kept it hid.'

No one in the room seemed to be breathing. They all knew what Vance was saying and watched Kimble closely. He was obviously deep in thought . . . and, suddenly, he knew it was up to him now.

'Well, it's all theory, seeing as no one knows where Madigan is – or even if he's still alive. I'll send in my report that you're not Madigan, Vance, as I thought. You're . . . too different to the man I'm looking for, but you're a damn lucky man, just the same.'

Vance held out his hand. They gripped firmly. 'I know it, Beau. I reckon Madigan'd be proud to call you his sidekick, right proud.'

'Maybe – or could be just what he'd expect of me. He lived by very strong codes, wouldn't deviate from them unless he could do it with a clear conscience. I suppose I could do a lot worse than be like him.'

'He'd be proud to know that.'

Kimble looked a bit flustered, then embarrassed as Merida lifted to her toes and kissed him lightly on his good cheek. 'Come back and be our best man, Beau.'

'I might just do that.' He handed Vance the message and the man read the last few lines, looked up sharply. Kimble smiled. 'Best get going. Have to start sometime.'

'Going to keep on looking, Beau?'

'Guess so – but a long way from here. I was steered wrong, but it's been good meeting you folks.'

'How long will you search, Beau?' asked Merida, a little anxiously, standing closer to Vance now.

Kimble shrugged. 'Chief's orders are plain enough.' He gestured to the message form Vance was still holding. 'I keep looking until I find him.' As he moved away, he said, 'I'm bound to run into him somewhere, sometime. . . .'

Merida called softly, 'I think he is a man who has earned some peace, Beau!'

He turned and looked over his shoulder at them, side by side with Vance's arm about Merida's slim waist. He smiled again.

'Yeah – who knows? The way things are, I may never find Madigan.'